.the
jewish son

•the
jewish son

a novel

DANIEL
GUEBEL

Translated by
JESSICA SEQUEIRA

SEVEN STORIES PRESS
new york • oakland • london

Originally published as *El hijo judío* by Literatura Random House, Buenos Aires, 2018.

First Seven Stories Press edition April 2023. Published by arrangement with Casanovas & Lynch Literary Agency, Barcelona, Spain.

Seven Stories Press
140 Watts Street
New York, NY 10013
www.sevenstories.com

College professors and high school and middle school teachers may order free examination copies of Seven Stories Press titles. Visit https://www.sevenstories.com/pg/resources-academics or email academics@sevenstories.com.

Library of Congress Cataloging-in-Publication Data

Names: Guebel, Daniel, 1956- author. | Sequeira, Jessica, translator.
Title: The Jewish son : a novel / Daniel Guebel ; translated by Jessica
     Sequeira.
Other titles: Hijo judío. English
Description: New York : Seven Stories Press, [2023]
Identifiers: LCCN 2022053234 | ISBN 9781644212899 (trade paperback) | ISBN
     9781644212905 (epub)
Subjects: LCGFT: Novels.
Classification: LCC PQ7798.17.U254 H5513 2023 | DDC
     863/.64--dc23/eng/20221216
LC record available at https://lccn.loc.gov/2022053234

Printed in the USA.

9 8 7 6 5 4 3 2 1

What we fear most always happens.
I write: may Thou have mercy. And now?
—CESARE PAVESE, *The Business of Living*

An anecdote can explain everything, if you don't forget what escapes it.

There wasn't any food I liked as a child. Salty and sweet tastes, liquid and solid textures, big and small servings—I found everything disgusting. Feeding me was a real chore. Something made it through my lips, of course, else I'd be dead, but my dissatisfaction also increased this risk of death. What was it I wanted, instead of what they were offering? I can't even say. Maybe, more than a whim, my pickiness was fury that I wasn't the only child anymore; I found my sister's birth indigestible.

Account for it any way you like, but my situation kept getting worse, so my parents took me to a pediatrician. He opted for the cold turkey approach: given that I was already eating so little, now I should be cut off from food entirely, until in my desperation I begged, oh please!, the error is mine, grant me the piece of bread I once scorned. The diet worked this way: Day One, total fast. Day Two, a single spoonful of tea, enriched with honey. Day Three, two spoonfuls. I don't know how long the progression was supposed to continue, but within the week my paternal grandmother intervened, turning up and preparing a chicken soup with rice, which she served in a deep hot plate on a metal stand. As she guided spoonful after spoonful of soup to my mouth, she murmured, "You have to eat until your plate is empty, there's something really lovely at the bottom." The spoon plunged into the stew with its grains of rice and thick layer of fat that had melted off the chicken skin, forming a layer along with the little pieces of carrot, potato, and onion, and as it resurfaced, loaded to the brim, overflowing with contents, it created a suction effect, the liquid hollowed out by the spoon rippling toward the edges of the plate in heavy wavelets, briefly allowing a glimpse of something like a mirage under the dense concoction, an outline or future revelation, the promise of what had been promised. Captain Nemo couldn't have felt greater anticipation than I did, plunging the prow of his *Nautilus* into the ocean for the first time. The imminence of knowledge, the possibility of accessing unexplored realms, presented itself. And then there he was before my eyes, a small Chinese gentleman printed on porcelain. He was bowing to a Chinese lady walking by, carrying a silk parasol she rested flirtatiously on her shoulder. I think that's all, and maybe there wasn't even a lady, just a man standing motionless, alone. Starting that moment, I began to eat the soup every day, the whole plate of it, to see the man appear wreathed in grains of rice, an edible filigree. The Chinese man was my first Eastern tale. From that moment, my childhood passion for the exotic would supply me with the nutrients I needed to survive in a world that failed to nourish my imagination. It must be said, in case it isn't yet clear—by that point anguish had already taken its toll on me, and its expression was a kind of painful rictus that upset my parents. No one quite knows what to do with a boy; his existence is forever an enigma. He destroys his elders' calm, ruins their emotional lives, burdens them with worries that are only alleviated in the days immediately preceding their own deaths, when their sons are themselves adults or almost old men, and the once-young parents, contemplating the horizons of the past, understand the cherished dreams and illusions they had for their offspring will be forever frustrated: deceptions. To accept this usually takes a couple of decades, in an effect of decantation that begins to accelerate with the end of adolescence. But in addition to all this, from a very early age I saw in my parents' eyes not just premature disenchantment and irritation, but also, or so I believed, a desire to see me vanish by way of some catastrophic miracle. A sunstroke on the beach, doubly assured by a collapse of the cliff where we picnicked, the stones hitting me square on the head; an automobile accident with myself as sole casualty; a timely kidnapping followed by my assassination and the sale of my organs; or a simple disappearance, reported in the police bulletin: "Kid gone up in smoke." Since this never happened, and I couldn't help but be who I was (or what I was), I fantasized about some kind of reparation, also miraculous, which would make them accept me by changing me into whomever—or whatever—they hoped I would be. Obviously I didn't know what or who that meant, even if I listened carefully to the names they called me ("crybaby," "pain in the ass") and adjectives they used to describe me ("insufferable," "clingy"), and started to think it would've been better had my grandmother let me die of hunger. But every essence persists in its being, and every being persists in its essence, with humans no exception. And so I made myself constant promises to reform, strived to be likable in the eyes of my parents, exerted myself in every possible way to survive and be accepted, even if I didn't know how to do so or why this was necessary. It's naïve to think love's constructions can triumph over the wear and tear of time's passing: what is not given, whole and from the start, is never given at all. I saw my efforts dash against the wall of my parents' bewilderment, as they took such attempts for impulses and eccentricities; but in consequence, instead of withdrawing to the solitude of my room, I threw myself once again into the struggle for love, multiplying my attempts in the belief that, eventually, I would pierce through the wall of incomprehension. I couldn't manage it. Everything became an offering that sought to procure the love denied to me, and I doubled down on my efforts to please. Yet time and again, receiving my father's icy gaze or my mother's apathy, I, who had gone toward them smiling and with open arms, had to draw back, questioning what the appropriate gesture or word should have been, and telling myself that since I hadn't achieved the miracle of love, I had to accept the responsibility for its rejection—in the form of both my original, irrevocable error and its logical consequence. "I'm an idiot, I must die," I told myself.

This might sound cruel to the reader; I was just a boy. But it was even crueler to speak these phrases to myself in the conviction I was grasping my parents' true message: "You're an idiot, you must die."

How could I bring about an end to that torment, and a beginning to acceptance, provisional as it might be? I tried to make myself tirelessly and constantly visible, with the aim that my mother and father would be unable to forget me for even a second. But the only thing this achieved was that my whole family united to claim I was jealous of my sister, whom they'd nicknamed "Chuchi" and called "precious little thing," "beauty," "loveliest teeny-tiny babykins conceived since humanity's inception." They exalted the porcelain tone of her little hands, her rosy cheeks, her perfectly modeled features, her chubby legs, her tantrums, grunts, babbles, vomits, defecations. Everything added to the charm of that little princess who stole attention from me, and who, to top it off, I was expected to celebrate too. And so I did, exaggerating my affection and concealing my spite, pinching her cheeks and hugging her whenever they passed her to me to hold. I hugged her with such enthusiasm she soon had to be wrenched away, to prevent suffocation. It's not that I didn't want to give her love. Just the opposite. Overcoming my first, brutal impulse to destroy her, I tried to offer care, and to be a real older brother, even as with small, secret torments I continued preparing her for the moment she'd be forced to embody the moral pain that I'd suffered, when the cycle of family fascination over her aura of novelty reached its end and neglect swept her into its mantle of denial.

Of course, it was still too early for this to happen, and in the meantime, Chuchi was the icon of the worshippers around her. The more she was adored, the more I dwindled in comparison. As my sister took her first steps, I was falling.

<hr />

And so the years slipped by, in that thrombosis of the affections, that stasis of a repeated dream. I grew up dry and hard as a reed, and my caprices and insolences began to adopt the form of hate, as a treacherous program of harm to others. In a preliminary diagram of the family architecture, my father was the strong one in the house, my mother the weak. In my politics of resentment, I decided to sabotage those links and test my mother's patience with the "thousand and one." To put it another way, I hoped to make the course of her days an inferno, with a thousand and one nights of nocturnal intimacy ruined through an accumulation of laments about my conduct, succeeded by reproaches from my father, who would accuse my mother of not leaving him in peace. That mode of operations revealed itself to be sterile and counterproductive, and if I'd possessed an ounce of cunning, I would have abandoned it immediately. Yet I pressed on with the assault, transforming myself into an unbearable element within an unbearable situation. And maybe there was a certain logic to this persistence, whose reaches I did not yet understand.

What were the "thousand and one" I inflicted on my mother? I jumped, I shouted, I smashed plates on the table, I didn't answer her calls, I refused to wash my hands, I played marbles all over the house then didn't pick them up (so others would step on them, slip and fall, break their necks), I pinched Chuchi . . . All an inventory of youthful treacheries that, according to my mother, cried out to the heavens for reprisal. But instead of immediately supplying me with a punishment equivalent to the dimensions of my offense—yanks on the ear, hair, or nose; slaps, smacks, or blows of her sandal—my mother warned me: "You'll get what's coming to you, when your father gets home." I shouted at her, I begged: "No, please, I want you to hit me." But my mother refused: "I won't be the one who does it, he'll be the one who lays down the law."

———

Franz Kafka's *Letter to His Father* is one of my favorite books. If I had to choose between rescuing this handbook of self-disparagement and reproach from a blazing fire, or *Ulysses*, I'd abandon Joyce's pyrotechnic novel to the flames and burn my fingers to save the few pages written by the Czech Jew. But that decision (soul over exhibitionism) does not blind me to the knowledge that, in the *Letter*, a perverse breeze blows. A naïve reading of the text might lead us to believe young Kafka is an innocent victim, as we identify with the injured tone of his prose suggesting a sensitive spirit at pains to explain to his father and himself who he is, knowing or believing we know that within the father, Don Hermann, abysses of brutality and incomprehension are hidden. In fact, Kafka didn't even have the courage to hand over the letter to his father, choosing instead to give it to his mother so she would know its contents and work as an intermediary, softening the irate response of the recipient as far as possible, or in the best of cases, serving as its translator. What the text constantly says is: that which I am, Father, you shall never understand. If you like, it is a testimony to the vast confusion woven by the threads of inheritance, proof of the absorbing sensation of strangeness a father always feels before the singularity and otherness of his progeny. Thinking in this way, it would make sense to ask the Christians, that is, the Jews with polytheistic inclinations, what they believe God experienced when his son, Jesus, decided to surrender himself in sacrifice to humanity. And it would also be interesting to find out what Jesus thought when confronted by the terrifying absence of the Father, who made a dash for the abyss without taking any measures to prevent a suicide by the Son. If Christianity, or Catholicism if you prefer, elevated the Virgin Mary (Miriam) to the highest celestial hierarchies, it is because she was understood as a necessary condition to explain the meaning of that sacrifice to God. Yeshua (whether ben Pandera, or not) required Miriam for this process to take place. But, as is also well known, a father is often incapable of understanding, since in him, far more than in the mother, it takes time for the consciousness to germinate the idea that the birth of a child inscribes, in the books of destiny, the date of one's own death. That delay is the true womb of punishment. And that is why Franz Kafka delivered the letter to his mother, so she would read it, and understand the sort of husband she had, and having grasped this, refrain from giving him the letter. Franz's mother, who understood everything immediately, did exactly this, and returned the pages to her son. Did she read the letter or not? I take it for granted that she did: that, in fact, she was the true recipient of the writing. The scene of the message's aborted delivery, and its return, with one false recipient and another true, completes the reading. Why would Don Hermann Kafka ever take upon himself the work of scrutinizing that inventory of lamentations and complaints? He was no more than a peasant who early on had stopped trying to understand a son sophisticated in his cultural decisions but clumsy in his sentimental ones, a scatterbrain incapable of giving him what he dreamed of: a grandson. A grandson to offer him solace and consolation in his final years.

When read as an adult, *Letter to His Father* awakens pity for the poor man who wore himself out lifelong to honorably provide for his family, and at the dawn of old age had to face the evidence he'd raised a weakling son, an emaciated vegetarian miser who hated him while feigning the greatest submission. I'd like to have had a father like him; it would have been much simpler. Instead, I . . . I, who hoped only for a little acceptance and respect and love, and who did not bear in my spirit the slightest desire to be rebuked, merited only blows. I highly doubt Don Hermann ever dared to raise a hand against Franz.

———

"Just wait until your father gets home, then you'll have a real treat," Mama said.

I begged her, "Please," I said, "You hit me right now, please." But she said, "No, you have to wait." Those situations produced the feeling of an imminence that took hours to be made concrete: a delayed anguish that unfurled over endless minutes, in anticipation of the punishment I implored her to execute straight away. "My Lord," I prayed, "give me every pain necessary, but in the present!" Ever since then, time has become for me the form assumed by the sinister, and life a prolonged investigation into the forms of enduring punishment. In suffering them, you discover how much you can tolerate without breaking, or if you do, what promises to interject, what requests for forgiveness, what pleas, what demonstrations of repentance: the number of times it is necessary to sink your knees into the earth.

My father. He came back from work each day, fed up with his labors. He opened the door (how much I feared that moment and those that preceded it, the squeak of the garage door, the muffled rumble of the entering car, the hum of the switched-off motor). His first question was always: "How did the kids behave today?" And then the response came: "With Chuchi I had no trouble, but he . . ." Without naming me, my mother started in on her list of infractions committed. Then my father raised his eyes to the sky, in a gesture that encapsulated his infinite fatigue, and with a slow hand he unloosened his belt, which came off him whistling like a snake. After pulling on the two ends to confirm the robustness of the strap, he raised it and said: "Come here." And before the first blow, he uttered a statement whose meaning for me constituted the greatest enigma: "This is going to hurt me more than it does you."

A belt isn't a knout or whip bristling with nails, and my father lashed me with the leather, never using the buckle to tear into me or strike my face. At the beginning of the session, he let fly his usual questions: "Why did you behave so badly, when are you going to start being a good boy . . . ?" Over the course of that interrogation, during which I begged him to stop the punishment, and offered no answers but sobs, the speed and intensity of the blows increased. I don't remember now if I remained standing during those moments, or if my father bent me over his knees and flogged me in that position. I doubt it was the latter, because in that case the operation would have been complicated by the proximity of the implement to the part of the body being struck. Thus I assume my father maintained a convenient distance, twisted his wrist and began with the strappings. Nor do I remember whether, after I pulled down my trousers, I stayed in my underwear, or whether my ass was exposed to the air. I don't need to spell out that the gradations of pain varied; since my father wore trousers with narrow loops, the width of the belt could not have exceeded five centimeters, and each blow thus necessarily fell upon a different area: his was not a methodical "sweep" of the totality but a partial intervention dictated by chance, at whose discretion the belt landed on new zones or applied itself entirely or partially to a zone already hit. Even worse than the strokes on the rear were the ones that fell on the legs or waist: they burned and stung with a hundredfold greater harshness. The tears surged forth of their own volition, involuntary liquid responses fired into the air that my father, since he was behind me and could not see my face, did not take into account as a sign he should stop. What's more, as the blows escalated in intensity, I shut myself away into the greatest silence, which he took to be a proof of resistance to his punishment or a protest against his convictions, and increased his fury. Under those circumstances, he lost track of his strength, or perhaps the rhythmic cadence made him enter into a disturbed state, and from a certain point onward, return became impossible. This was the point he saw himself driven to reach. Then he not only yelled, but from the corner of his lips a foam began to emerge, which flew into the air in sputtering droplets. It's true that this happened on only a few occasions, since the majority of times he stopped beforehand, either because he retained a sliver of consciousness, or because of Chuchi, who interrupted at her own risk and more than once received a couple of blows intended for me. My sister would let out a shriek, and say: "Stop it, Dad, you're going to kill him!" Then he would emerge from his frenetic dream, refrain with a shudder, and hurry to lock himself away in the matrimonial bedroom. Through the closed doors we could hear his crying, a soft, convulsive, anguished moan from a strangled throat.

After that, my mother, who had first betrayed me, then not known how to interrupt or extract me from the punishment, would pull up my trousers and say: "Go apologize to your father. Just look how much he suffers, because of you."

I don't remember or don't want to remember if there was ever a time when I did that, and asked his forgiveness for making him punish me. What I do remember or now reconstruct is the hate I felt, since even in pain my father stole the scene. Hate and disgust for his abject reduction to spasmodic infernos, and his childish impulse to excuse himself by means of tears, after having submitted a real child to adult violence. Today I even believe it should have been I who raised the belt to whip him until he bled, exonerating him from weakness until he released the bile produced by acceptance of his wife's mandate. Maybe he never understood that he was merely the instrument with the strength sufficient to dole out the lashing actually given to us by my mother.

The only brave person in the family was my sister, who stepped in to save me.

——•——

I wrote "hate." But at heart it wasn't hate I felt, but pity. For my father, because he'd become a stranger, and for myself, because to him I was an unknown species. In this aspect, yes, I should have asked his forgiveness. For not being the way he wanted me to be, for not having known how to win his love, even his mercy. At the same time, even then, in those waves of humiliation that washed over me when confronting the insignificance of my own being, I understood that despite it all, I wasn't guilty for failing to measure up. If my father had dreamed of a son he could take pride in, a son different from what I was and would always be, there was nothing he could do, since his ideal design lacked form: deception is a completely negative experience, and offers no model of opposition. And yet . . . and yet within me I did cherish a certain hope, a fantasy so modest it seemed unconnected to the illusions of a boy who consoled himself with dimensions of the fantastic. My hope fulfilled itself as a dream that occupied my waking hours with the persistence of a hallucination.

In the dream my father carried me in his arms, while my mother held Chuchi. All of us stood in front of the bathroom mirror in our home. We looked in the mirror, we looked at ourselves. My father was smiling, serene, and so was my mother. After a few seconds of silence, in that peace, my father spoke to my image, saying: "Until this moment you were an idiot without even knowing it, but starting now, you'll be as normal as the rest." And that is all. Nothing in particular happened, there was no magical sound or glimmer of harps to mark a change in consciousness or difference I could recognize between the previous state and current one. There was no new world. All that happened was that, with the dissipation of my webs of idiocy, my parents accepted me. Maybe the effect was illusory: my normality was on the other side of the mirror, while the real me continued to be the same idiot as ever. Since the scene stopped there, it was impossible to delve to the bottom in search of an explanation, as with the hot plate of soup my grandmother brought me.

It would be easy now to claim that amidst such neglect in life, I clung to literature for lack of anything else, or anything better.

But better or worse, here, are meaningless terms. I chose to be a writer, if it's something you can choose, and abided by the decision. The obsessive impulse with which I confronted my task, the consciousness of being nobody except someone who writes (of being nobody if I did not write) had its consequences: being a writer always does damage. But to become a writer was, for me, an act of reparation. An image persisted before me, even if just in the mirror, after my family's dissolving act. It wasn't me, but it also wasn't an illusion; it was something that existed in its own right, something external to me that, even so, defined me. The secret nucleus of my activity harbored a tremendous ambition. "You're normal now," my father had told me. Yet that wasn't enough, it didn't compensate for all those years as an idiot. It was necessary to make amends for my deficient origin. What sense did it make to compensate for time lost with normality? None. I believe in the importance of small origins, since it's there that everything converges, and lost paradises can exist with the condition you recuperate them in transfigured form. My grandmother saved me from death by starvation by telling me a story, one that simultaneously vanished and revealed itself through the figure of a hidden Chinese man. Perhaps in memory of that act of love, I've written fiction and books centered around "exotic" themes, even if more than a few consider these to be frivolous subjects rather than nourishing material. In the same way, when in my repeated dream I converted to a normality of being, my years of idiocy or previous subnormality still had to be corrected by another route, since it was impossible to dream I'd been a nonidiot, in a reverse process that carried me from the scene in the mirror toward my own birth. That route, too, was literature. And the complete reparation of that fracture, that deficit of years, had to be operated by means of a compensation whose achievement was the most impossible of impossibles: starting as an idiot, I had to end in greatness. (Idiocy returns at the very moment you stop fleeing from it.)

A digression: the last time I saw Rodolfo Enrique Fogwill, in one of his attacks of malevolence, he said to me: "You don't have many ideas." My answer was: "Like Kafka, who had just one. You, on the other hand, have an unlimited number of ideas, which is why you write so much nonsense." Truth is, I said nothing, I'm not quick on my feet with responses, but it's what I thought. Since our next contact was by telephone, and he was delirious in those two or three days before he died, it didn't seem appropriate to impose on him, in his agony, the understanding of something you must learn alone: that there comes a moment when the illusion of proliferating diversity surrenders its mask, and you commit to a monotonous resolve, the impulse of delving your spade into the rich exploration of a single subject, to find the secret bone, the inert material, that sustains the impulse of your writing. Well then. For years I sought the diversity that would multiply me in the mirrors of those I fled, seeking to avoid the lash of destructive words (for instance, "You were an idiot and will be one so long as you live, each day a little more, until you choke to death on your babble and drool"). I wanted to be the kind of writer who proposes something different, who becomes different, with every book. That impulse didn't respond to an act of the will. It was as if my writing embodied the spirits of writers I didn't know, as a parasitic immortality, an acceptable formula for joy. Yes, sometimes I do feel happy writing, and if I keep on like this to the end, I'd say that my life has had some purpose. It's clear this doesn't happen all the time, of course. You also have to work to eat. And you have to take care of loved ones, in those pathetic moments before their death.

   Did I write "hate"? That's not the right word. My mother was a creature who never knew what she was doing. When instead of disciplining errors at the moment of my transgression (with the possible discipline being a mere reproach or sweet caress), she delegated the administration of justice to my father's hands, what she was doing was admitting her difficulty in confronting the problems of raising her children. Rather than face the challenges herself, she chose to submit to the masculine authority in whose veneration she'd been educated. In this way, by abstaining from doing anything that would prevent my father's beatings, she not only confirmed the validity of a process she'd begun with her own complaint, but also revealed the way that the course of events could spill out of control: my mother didn't protect me out of fear that my father, blind with fury, would end up striking her too. Her. At no moment did it cross her mind that she could have averted what happened, which according to what she told me years later, horrified her. Nor did she draw any conclusions from the evidence my sister produced upon stepping forward in my defense: that my father let up at the first external intervention. In reality, my father had been expecting this. It freed him from the burden of having to dole out punishment. In his own childhood, he had received his share. The chain of generations. Once I asked my grandfather how his own father had treated him. "Like a dog," he said. "What does that mean?" I asked. "He hit me on the back with a stick," he said, "until I blacked out."

I'm wasting my life if I can't write anything. I should let my nails grow out and sink them into the wood of this desk. Better yet my teeth. But obviously one can't write that way. Idiot. Idiot. Enough of this. A few months ago, I saw some old black and white photos snapped by my uncle Alberto: My father and I are running through a park, my father's holding me, I'm sitting on the hood of our Peugeot 403, we're laughing. My mother wears glasses with sequins and a fake pearl necklace, and she's smiling. What kind of a sinister story am I telling?

An anecdote can explain everything, if you add back what escapes it.

I'm going to see my father at the clinic where he is hospitalized. Not for the prostate cancer, which advances slowly at his age, but for the cysts on his bladder. The IV and catheter have been removed, his urine is no longer dark red. He looks better, though he still complains every time he pisses. He's sitting on a chair, wearing only an adult diaper, extra-large. His waistline and belly swelled after a couple meters of intestine full of burst diverticula were cut away from him, in a surgery. For a few months his anus looked unnatural, and every time I changed the colostomy bag, I had to clean up the shit that had accumulated at the edges of the wound. A semi-liquid secretion, a paste with acidic humidity that burned his skin. He required two or three failed operations before the digestive tube could be reconnected without leaking. The diverticula are nasty little devils: a few years before this, just after he turned eighty, he suffered from intestinal bleeding that resulted in low blood pressure and an oxygen imbalance in the brain, producing a cerebrovascular episode that left him with delays of expression and comprehension. "You

could've ended up a lot worse, as one of those hunched gee-
zers who dribble all over themselves," I told him. It's true he
understands and thinks with greater lucidity than he is able to
express. Sometimes I ask how he is, and he raises his hands to
the height of his temples and flaps them while making a sound
with his mouth. This must be the sound in his head, related
to the cerebral burst that prevents him from settling ideas
into words he can communicate. I witness how he endures
his losses. He maintains his dignity as far as he's able, even
if he sometimes still pisses himself when he needs the toilet.
His only revenge is to bully the nurses: to accept that they're
cleaning his ass must be harder than taking a shit on them. He
asks me what we're doing in this clinic, and why we don't take
him home, to his home. He doesn't remember pissing short
streams of blood that spilled over his balls, because he was
unable to grab hold of his penis and stretch it. He looks out
the window, touches his belly, and says something like: "The
hansan of disbridor." "I can't understand you, Dad," I say. I
take apart and recombine the words, try to figure out whether
he means hand or sane or ruin or bridge or disorder. I ask him
to repeat the phrase. He does, but it doesn't change. "I don't
understand," I repeat, and he smiles and shrugs. Sometimes
I ask him who I am, and he says: "You." When I ask what his
name is, he says: "Me." Then I play multiple choice: "Am I
Aníbal?" "No." "Alberto?" "No." "Marcos?" "No." "Miriam?"
He laughs, "No." I say my name. "That one, yes. That's you."
He knows that as long as he gets it right, and we recognize
this, he'll keep living in his own house, instead of a dump
for old folks. And he knows that the names and meanings of
things stay fixed, even when everything else goes spinning.

The blood stopped flowing, the urine turned yellow again. He went to the clinic for his bleeding, and left the clinic when it stopped. A prostate tumor was the cause, but at his age it doesn't make sense to consider an operation, except if the bleeding repeats and is uncontrollable. Nor is it worth battling his cancer with a hormonal medication that decreases testosterone, weakens the bones and muscles, and boosts the growth of mammary glands. The ambulance crosses the city with its siren song, my father tied to the gurney. When the nurses unload him at his house, he goes straight to bed, dragging his feet. I tell him I'm leaving. "When will you come back?" he asks. "Tomorrow," I say. "Not today?" I tell him goodbye with a kiss, but he wants two, one on each cheek. Like the Russians. The fact that the man who struck a boy is today the old man who clings to life thanks to his adult children's efforts does not give me the slightest satisfaction. Rather, a muffled pain. We've spent our lives trying to be better as children to him than he was as a father to us, but there's no solace in it: we can no longer resist the evidence that soon he'll die.

What to do?

As a child, I asked myself this question with the intention of resolving my family situation. Since I didn't yet know how to interpret the kind of alliance established between my mother and father, which was articulated in the form of a punishment for their son, and since I hadn't yet discerned the role of my mother in the situation and believed her to be another victim, I attributed the complete authority of abuse to my father. What to do to survive was therefore equated for me, at that time, with a self-interrogation about how to read my father's mind, to discover a valve that could shut off the tap of violence; and about how I might effect a reconciliation that transformed his feeling for me into, if not love, at least acceptance, or if that was also impossible, then simple forgiveness, for the error of having been born. I wanted to find, within hell, the place where there was no hell, and help it to grow, and make a home there. Not because such places didn't exist in reality (I could go out into the street to play with people in the neighborhood, and friends from school, and fellow club members, as my fantasies about the future bloomed), but because my experiences were affected by my father's scrutiny. More than once he proved he knew even the slightest of my offenses in detail, and his boasting about the perfection with which he administered his systems of control led me to believe, in a delirium of total invention, that he'd installed a vast empire of surveillance, impossible to locate and dismantle. Even when he was trying to be thoughtful and reasonable, and would sit down for a talk with me, speaking to me directly, saying he'd help me fix this or that aspect of my behavior, creating the fiction of affectionate dealings between us, what I observed was less a pedagogical, corrective impulse than an insistence on criticizing the very structure of my self-hood: I read those appeals for reform as signs of his desire to annihilate me. I perceived criticism and rejection even in this gentle method (the harsh one was the whip). But luckily, at the margin of what was correct or mistaken about my interpretation, and distinct from the question of what would encourage his best intentions, I was also able to build a kind of shell to protect myself from verbal abuse, an effect of the determination of my being to survive despite everything. Even today it's hard for me to understand how my being was able to tuck itself away, asleep or growing like a quiet moss as it clung to the rocks of life, through those formative years when my only resources were tears or flight from harassment by the enemy singing songs of death. Nor do I feel the need to resolve this metaphysical mystery in abstract terms, as the countermeasures I adopted were practical ones. In the moments when my father sat me down so we could talk, man to man, face to face, I, who already knew the appeal beforehand and could anticipate his rhetoric, the points he would stress, the invocations of my presumed ability to display better behavior (invocations that didn't propose any happy or comforting future, but in the very notion of improvement concealed a utopian summit), began to sense my own growing distance from the scene, as a kind of perceptual alteration. My father was speaking, but his words reached my ears transformed into pure sound, a sound that lacked intonation, musicality, sense. Those words didn't refer to anything, even if by forcing him to separate his lips to modulate them, they also forced the rest of his body to carry out a series of movements of persuasive intention, gesticulations that led him to use his hands, tilt his head to one side then another, or bend over and straighten his back. My attention concentrated on these phenomena of transformation, trivial yet absorbing: His face began to shine with a kind of emission of yellow light, which rose up within him and glowed from his skin, and this was accompanied by a parallel increase in the size of his head. First the cranial covering began to spread and expand in width, then the ears pulled the temples toward them, and then the rest of the face began to stretch too, each particular feature amplifying in size, before my father's whole head at last turned into a shiny balloon that fluttered and shrank and swelled without detaching itself from the rest of his body.

Of course, these defensive means were short-lived. I'd only just begun to observe these new expressions of his character when the technique stopped working, and once again I was left unarmed and wary, assaulted by a series of reproaches about my failure to study as much as I should, about my responsibility in fights with Chuchi ("You're the older brother and should be ashamed to treat her like that"), about my poor conduct which made my mother suffer ("She doesn't know what to do with you anymore"). It was the dawn of adolescence, and this verbal artillery now substituted for thrashings, perhaps anticipating the moment when I'd be old and strong enough to refuse to take them. Even so, because the terror had lived within me for so long, his hand continued to figuratively rise up and float in the air. The evolution of pain inflicted during a punishment requires that when the blows are suspended, a new stage be inaugurated with relation to the punisher, a fragile alliance or bridge toward a situation where bodies no longer shudder or voices tremble, so that in the course of time, a lasting agreement might be signed to compensate for the effects of pain and resentment, and possibly enable the formation of new germs of friendship or love. Yet the memory of past time corrodes this ideal from within, since behind the cracks there is hidden suffering, which knows belief to be an illusory refuge, and hope of change a useless dream, and merely adds new pain to the experiences already lived.

Even after my father ceased to strike me, I'd been hit enough times to assume that their replacement by a series of warnings anticipated a punishment of greater intensity, a more sophisticated administration of damage. In every "good intention" of my father's, there quivered a threat whose system of organization and syntax I had to dismantle as a precaution against unhappy futures. And so I buried myself in the non-verbal signs and tones my father used, trying to distinguish the shades of increasing complexity within them. My form of reading was pure attribution, which boiled down the whole series of events to a single phrase: "You don't know how or when this truce will end, and eventually you will be punished again, in a new form."

I've always been fascinated by machines with visible gears that untwist screws, turn pulleys, slide ball bearings, or eject steam, at the same time as they give an account of their own operations: independent of the production of objects, stripped of the criterion of utility, seemingly free of fatigue. Machines that promise to last longer than the universe that contains them, but will cease to work when the universe itself shrinks and crushes them. This fascination can, in a certain way, be equated with the minor mechanism of visual distortion I used to remove myself from my father's hurtful words, even if true extraction only came later. The real mechanism was the situation that trapped me, the one operated by my father and mother that led to their behavior with me. A mechanism of terror. It took me years before I could appreciate its functioning, its delicate game of replacements and substitutions. In fact, I'm not sure even now that I understand it completely, or am capable of describing it (which is why I prefer to think about machines). What I do understand is that I was necessary for it to be put into motion, though I was neither the cause nor the necessary condition of its perpetuation, just as the appearance of the little bird that says cuckoo in old windup clocks is superfluous to the clock's act of stating the hour.

As I explained, my poor behavior as a child produced not an immediate penalty by my mother, but the threat of a punishment delayed in time and executed with infinite weariness by my father. Now then: Basic logic would suggest that if I'd behaved well (whatever that means), the prompt complaints of my mother—which I took as betrayals—would evaporate like morning dew. But I'm convinced that even if a temporary pretext for my bad behavior had not existed, it wouldn't have been hard for them to find another, and so the mechanism of abuse could always replicate itself. My father went to work in the mornings like a normal citizen who sells the effort of his physical and intellectual work in exchange for a living, and at night looks for a way to relieve the pressure accumulated over the course of the day. It must be recognized that this unburdening took place within certain limits: although they hurt, his beltings didn't leave physical marks. But naturally the violence, regulated by the interventions of my sister Chuchi, produced effects on the family, above all on my father himself, who ended up convinced that power always devolved back to his hands (to his lash). This conviction received further nourishment from a source of another order: we were living under a military government, and my father belonged to a political organization proscribed by Law 17.401, written by the dictatorship. For safety's sake, members of his party kept their condition hidden, which was of course detrimental to the spread of their ideology. To top it off, a wave of persecutions and arrests left behind only a small core group of members, faithful to the revolutionary cause. It was this enlightened avant-garde of iron protectors that would illuminate the path, when the necessary conditions were given for the development of proletarian consciousness. My father, behind the appearance of an insignificant manager at a household appliance firm, saw himself as one of the enlightened beings capable of changing the course of humanity: and in a triple transvaluation of values, he also turned our family's madness into a social ethic.

Since there's no way to transform the world if the will to do so doesn't first work its influence upon each transforming agent, the political mysticism that began to exercise its hypnosis over my father spread to the entire family. I imagine the process to be a kind of personal glorification, a radiance of which even my mother must have been aware. Whatever the case, and with a divine unconsciousness, since she neither realized her condition as manipulator nor fully assumed the position of victim, she went about adjusting to her role as the selfless wife who adores her revolutionary hero, and is incapable of doing anything but submit to his tyranny. In terms of "values," the scale of the family balance tipped ever more toward the side of my father. The entire spotlight of attention fell upon him. If he delayed too long returning home, my mother grew nervous. Of course her husband's late arrivals, whose reasons could be traced to clandestine meetings and security protocols, supplied me with an unhoped-for benefit, since by the time of his return I was already in bed, and given the late hour, punishment was deferred.

Was it one, ten, a hundred, a thousand, a million times my father hit me? I don't know. Maybe I'm inventing the repeated existence of a scene that never occurred, to exaggerate the baroque nocturnal parties of a childhood nourished by the horrors of my soul. Maybe that violence was a mental elaboration spun out of the fantasies of my mother, who must have desired as much as feared that her husband would be punished by police forces, with doses of violence more efficient and scientific than the blows I claim to have suffered. How is it possible for a child to know the hidden corners of the maternal mind, to the point of appropriating them and turning them into the very material of his psyche, until they become more real than any reality? It might seem strange, but the explanation is simple: I went about unveiling those secrets slowly, learning her language in silence and at my own cost, as like a sponge I absorbed the juices of her malaise.

"Shikse," "schvartze," "Unser Verter."

At the expanded table on Sundays, which served as the family's central committee, Spanish was occasionally swapped out for a dialect of the diaspora, a mixture of old German, Hebrew, Latin, and French. The replacement seemed to answer to a formula of courtesy: the young adults (my parents and uncles) turned to this other tongue to ease communication with their elders, for whom Spanish was a second language, and its use not as natural. My maternal grandmother, for example, could never say "egg." "Dañele, do you want me to make you a fried boibo?" she'd ask me, unable to pronounce "huevo." In childhood, these difficulties filled me with embarrassment and were like signs they belonged to a community external to the nation, something my classmates took it upon themselves to point out in primary school when they accused me of having killed Christ, a slander I defended myself from by shouting: "It wasn't me, it wasn't me!" The poor devils must have believed that Joshua was Christian, and been unaware that his rabbin-ical-messianic activity was inscribed within the ample Jewish tradition of mama's boys who believe themselves to be chosen for a very special destiny, a dream that adult life cruelly smashes against reality. In any case, it's enough to see how the Anointed One met his end: by hanging on a cross. But since this isn't about the life and sufferings of the son of God, but about mine, and I am the crucified one within closest reach, I'll return to my subject: on the walls of my neighborhood at the time—San Andrés, San Martín, province of Buenos Aires—three kinds of street graffiti flourished. The first, which seemed to contain an erotic message, was repeated block after block, a letter *P* that inserted its lower end into the opening of a short *V*. The second consisted of a series of brief declarations ("Mirta slut, Julio César cuckold," "Framini-Anglada, Perón in the Casa Rosada," "Olelé, Olelao, Cacho sucks, Alfonso puts out"). The third was limited to advertisements or direct incitements. I remember a few examples. One said: "Let the children come to me. I'll give them a weapon and teach them to hate their fellow men." Signed: "Communism." Another, already worn away by the years: "Be a patriot. Kill a Jew. Frondizi sold out to the Jews." Reading these, I worked out that my family and I were in danger for at least two reasons. And later, I discovered there was a double motive for the adults to use Yiddish. When they sent me to Jewish school (even though it would have been more useful to learn English, French, German, Italian, Chi-nese, Japanese, even Voynichese . . .), I learned that "shikse" meant non-Jewish woman and "schvartze" black, two ways of referring to the housemaid, while "Unser Vater" (the correct pronunciation), which could be translated as "Our Word," was the title of the official press bulletin of the Communist Party. The use of dialect was thus a way to keep children at the margin of adult themes, especially when these implied limits to safety.

The garage door of the house was high, made of sheet metal. Now and then my father would wake up at dawn, to cover with fresh paint the messages dripping in black tar that denounced us. "Bolshie commie Jews, get out of San Martín, our country, this planet."

My own understanding of what this meant took the form of concealment: it was necessary to hide or disguise ourselves. "Henpecked," my father called me, because I insisted on clinging to the refuge of my grandmothers' and mother's broad skirts, those devalued sites of feminine love, rather than identifying myself with him, the revolutionary hero who didn't know how to raise his weak and weepy son, a dark freckled runt who shut himself away in the bedroom to read. If I know something of the nooks and crannies of the feminine psyche, it's a knowledge that has come to me effortlessly, simply from having lived amongst women. But this knowledge was incomplete, since it only moved in one direction, with my mother oblivious to the existence of my wisdom. If she'd been capable of getting into my mind, as I did into hers—if she'd even conceived of such a possibility—my childhood years would have been easier. But the path had to be circuitous. When she left me alone and helpless, faced with mistreatment, I had to search for a way to protect myself, delving into the moral and mental nature of my father. But there, an even greater difficulty appeared: he presented himself to me

as the wall of walls, and within him were condensed both violence and mystery. In that early stage of life, I wasn't yet aware
of the degree of his participation in the political struggle for a
more just, equal society, but I did notice that his absences and
latenesses formed part of the construction of an identity more
meritorious than his wife's. And so, even if my initial impulse led
me, to seek refuge in my mother's skirts, another of an opposite
nature drove me to seek his approval. When my father rejected
me, I spun like a whirligig, clueless about how to win a place, a
minimum of approval in this world. What to do? A problem that
has kept philosophers awake since the Middle Ages, and which
my father's greatest idol claimed to have resolved, that is, Vlad-
imir Ilyich Ulyanov, Lenin.

I tried everything to win my father's affection. By turns I
was sullen and melancholy, or vitalist and frenzied. I tried to
interest myself in his tastes and enthusiasms (archaeology, pur-
sued as the gathering of Indian arrowheads while on holiday;
visual arts; domestic repairs; the preparation of cloyingly sweet
desserts). I celebrated his jokes, I listened to his anecdotes from
work, I furnished evidence of my decision to turn into the
person he desired. I suppose this will toward self-negation was
taken by my father as a sign of weakness, and simply became
further proof that all I merited was scorn. Of course, I exaggerate. If things had been precisely as I'm telling them, I'd be
long dead. But only hyperbole, what is stressed to the point
of excess (in this case, pain) can bring truth to light. Maturity
and a balanced point of view are part of a criminal policy to
encourage the settling for mediocrity in life. Exaggeration, by
contrast, intensifies and saves. I myself exaggerated a zealous
adherence to my father's decisions, to avoid the devastation of

my being that would accompany his indifference. The question of whether my attitude was erroneous, and I should have adopted open rebellion, making myself into somebody who was worth something, is a different matter. The fact is, I did rebel, but only outside the house. At school I was the complicated kid, the one with "behavioral problems." Faced with the slightest display of inconsiderateness or lack of affection by school authorities (teachers, principals, doormen), I yelled, kicked the doors, surrendered to attacks of fury, or made attempts to escape and go home, which led to visits with the principal, tests at the educational psychologist's office . . . "You act out to draw attention," he told me, year after year. Now there's a surprise! But why didn't he ask the reason I was doing it? The behavior of a child is an unknown language for the adult who thinks that to evaluate is the same as to resolve.

His place. "I'm sad," he tells me. I say he should draw, sketch lines, or make versions of doves or other things with tempera or crayon. He doesn't even take pleasure in looking at the flowers in the garden anymore. He only sinks his gaze into the ground, or watches what I'm doing. I'm watering the plants scorched by heat, and for a moment, as a joke, I think of hosing him down so he revives or gets angry or at least has some reaction, but I don't do it because his drawings would get wet. He looks at me, smiles and says: "You're crazy," as if anticipating my gesture. As if he knows what I'm thinking, at the exact moment I think it.

It's always been like this. Part of his analysis of my behavior, as I was describing above, was based on a knowledge of facts

I thought I'd kept hidden, as if he'd organized a system of surveillance that recorded each one of my steps, discerned the reasons for my actions, and delivered him a complete report about the state of my mental activity. To know everything about me seemed to produce a great satisfaction in him, which displayed itself as a half smile. To extend the comparison, I was a fish battling against the current in search of a vanishing point, and he was a system of precautions and anticipations which assumed the physical form of a net. Anything I could hope for—reserve, discretion, privacy—was caught and gutted in advance. Yet what mattered most to him wasn't even to give a contradictory opinion about any subject that involved me, but rather to let me know that he had detailed firsthand information about it. With this absolute knowledge produced by superior vision, he seemed to warn me, he could dominate every dimension of my future, and from my side he thus expected supreme acceptance and complete resignation. Again, I might be inventing. But if what I'm saying is true, such a scheme would annihilate the redemptive character of my mirror fantasy, in which his word could liberate me from idiocy. Even so, within the infinite extension of his domain, it was perhaps still possible to take refuge in some area that escaped his gaze, either because his system of surveillance had limitations, or because even the strictest of empires needs to maintain an area of simulated freedom, so that those condemned to hell are convinced there is a zone that is not hell, and are relieved from the burning of the flames, even temporarily, by the illusion they will be able to make this zone survive: by tending to it, by caring for it so that it grows, by helping it to survive and flourish.

For me, the sphere that was forever pushing to expand, forever on the point of bursting, was and continues to be literature. Maybe my father could see into my mind or deduce my actions from my thoughts. What he was incapable of doing, thanks to the speed and intensity with which I submerged myself in book after book, as soon as I learned how to read, was pursue me through that territory.

"Bananas," he says. "You're going bananas?" I ask. "Yes." "What's going on, Dad?" He lowers his head, raises his hands, and moves them as if twisting a screw, so it penetrates through the bones of his skull deep into the labyrinths of his brain. Then he points the index figure of his right hand, like a gun, and shoots. "Do you want to die?" "Yes." "Do you want someone to kill you?" "Yes." "Do you want to kill yourself?" "Yes." "Do you want me to get you a pistol?" "Yes." "Loaded with bullets or water?" He laughs. He looks at the ground.

A vocation subjects you to its consequences. As soon as I knew I wanted to be a writer, I lost my talent for drawing, school became a forced march through the desert of ennui, and the seclusions of reading hijacked the charms of adventure and open-air sports. The process wasn't a calm one: I raged against the loss of my possibilities, against the reduction of my life and its condensation into printed symbols. The discovery of the arbitrary condition of language was a private tragedy. It happened on an ordinary day, in summer. I was at the house of my maternal grandparents, and on the table was an oilcloth covering. For a while I entertained myself, tracing the geometrical motifs of its pattern. At some point, I felt hot—the skin on my arm, resting on the tablecloth, had begun to stick to the material—and I wanted to pour myself a glass of Refres-Cola and soda water. I reached out a hand and was about to grab the bottle of concentrated syrup, when all at once it struck me that the relation between objects and the words designated for them was not, as I'd assumed until then, an essential one. The glass container called "glass" could be "murta" or "rawxckgra"; the Refres-Cola, "xangu" or "kañdjfdikd"; the soda water, "hdkdlal"; and the water and the bubbles of gas that composed it, "kdaljdfkl" and "ieuryrtn," respectively. When I perceived this fracture, my world trembled. If each element of the totality was defined and delimited in a random way, then the reality of the universe itself dissolved, or at least its illusion of wholeness. When I discovered this, I felt an abyss open before my feet. It's curious, because in my place another child might have discovered a fount of unsuspected richness in the combinatorial possibilities offered by the arbitrary relation between words and things (and in the concentric discovery that a word is also a thing, arbitrarily constituted by smaller units); maybe for him, this would have inspired an exploration of the rhythmic, sonorous, syntactic capacities of each language. By contrast, it led me to cling to the edge of the precipice of my own language. To read, write, and speak only in Spanish became a way of renouncing the legacy of my elders and forging a path of my own (if I didn't speak Yiddish, I'd be less Jewish, more Argentine). It was also a wager, destined beforehand to failure, to fix

a single name to each object, as a result of its use. But now that
the rift was open, other evidence filtered through its crack; or
maybe the evidence came prior to this discovery, and was what
motivated it. During breaks at school, students in the upper
grades would amuse themselves by "planting the seed" in the
minds of those in lower grades about the method by which
the human species conceives, and the way the female egg is
courted by millions of sperm until one sperm at last manages
to cross through the plasma membrane and produce fertiliza-
tion. That scenario pointed to a million possible swarming
identities desperate to exist, which ultimately hurtled into a
void of nothingness after a single sperm accomplished its mission. Such waste gave me vertigo, and also let me peek into the
enormous abyss of chance that informed those wild dances of
heated corpuscles, and enabled the conquest of the maternal
egg by the sperm that bore my features. I'd experienced enormous luck in having defeated millions of rivals. But at the same
time, this achievement proved that my own existence was not
the effect of a clear, distinct, unique decision—the desire of
my parents to have me—but was instead the search for a son
or daughter in any form, a human being capable of occupying
that place. Judging by the way they treated me, it was clear
that they weren't totally satisfied with the result. In any case,
the almost infinite series of elements that had combined for
me to exist with my name, my primary and secondary physical
features, and my precise historical time, country, and family,
was contingent and not determined, random and not essential.

To write thus implied a decision to close the hiatus, to
develop a method that would give a personal trajectory and
unique pattern to the oilcloth on the table, whose identity was

still anonymous and whose signature might have belonged to any other.

With the relationship between names and things broken, the world continued to vibrate in terrifying possibility, but I clung with greater assurance to the edge of its precipice: I'd decided to be what I was. Even if, as I would soon realize, this meant paying a price.

My father had a friend named Julio, maybe his best friend. During the dictatorship, he was kidnapped and murdered by the police. I called him uncle. We went for lunch one day. I don't know why my father brought me along; I couldn't have been more than seven years old, and the topics of conversation went over my head and bored me to tears, though at the same time I tried to show an interest appropriate to the well-mannered young man they considered me to be. Over dessert there was a moment of silence, and then, without anything anticipating it, Julio looked at me through his coke-bottle glasses and asked the classic question: "What do you want to be when you grow up?" I, who already knew and believed nothing in the world could change my decision, felt the impulse to answer the truth straight away to impress him ("What a precocious boy, so young and he already knows what he wants"). But at the very same moment, a counterimpulse prevented me from speaking, since like an imperative that brooks no dissent, a more complete and complex idea had begun to form in my mind of my own vocation, accompanied by the conviction that if I spoke it out loud, by an order no one had forced me to carry out, which I alone was imposing upon myself, I would regret it for the remainder of my days. I made an attempt to keep hold of my freedom, and said what was true: "I am going to be a writer," but the phrase had barely passed through my lips before, to my own horror, this just-opened space of liberty vanished, as the weight of the imperative forced me to add: ". . . if my dad lets me." Julio laughed. My father did too, a couple seconds later. They were adults, long distant from the days of filial obedience. "Why 'if he lets you'? And if your dad doesn't let you, then what?" Julio asked. Since the unnecessary had now been said, through a trap I'd set for myself, it would have been absurd to reply: "Even if he doesn't let me, I'm still going to become a writer." So I turned red, face burning, and stayed quiet. Thus searing humiliation into the moment.

Was that tragic reply, my way of embarrassing myself, a kind of offering placed before the altar of my father, unnecessary, like all offerings? Or did my father need it to pretend that what I'd said surprised him? Who can say. All I know is that it faithfully adhered to our model of functioning, by which he, after a painful delay of his smile—producing it immediately would have showed my phrase was absurd, that I was and always would be free to choose—adopted a pained expression of surprise, showing an unexpected weakness of spirit or late understanding of the way he was ruining my life. Of course, these interpretations begin from a hypothesis: that my father faked surprise at my response, so that Julio would preserve respect for him. Truth is, I don't actually remember him wincing at that moment, since ashamed of myself, and the despicable position in which my response had left me, I didn't take my eyes off the ground.

Sunday lunch table. The meal goes on and on, but I eat quickly, get my fill early on, and find the after-dinner conversation unbearable. I want to go into the street to play, or run around the patio. Anything. But to do that, I have to get permission. I have to ask: "Dad, may I be excused?" He denies my request. And I remain seated, bored beyond belief. A while later I repeat the question again, and my father repeats the negation. Only after the third, fourth, maybe fifth time does he answer: "You can't be excused for how much you've eaten, but if you can hoist all that up, go on then."

The game repeats week after week. As the days go by, I forget the nature of his "pardon," and everything starts again. His approach of delaying mercy toward my irritating requests fills me with bitterness, until I at last receive his authorization, which he grants with a laugh. But over and over, I forget to hold on to my hate.

Another anecdote. Someone gives my father a dog, or he buys one, or finds one in the street. It's a mixture of German shepherd and some unknown breed. He brings the dog home as a puppy, and my sister and I immediately fall in love with the creature. We kiss him on the head (never the jaws or wet nose); we play with him; we run so he chases us. He's a joyful and carefree creature, at least until he grows up. My father tries to awaken his guardian instinct. He pretends to attack him, bark at him, and Wolf jumps back with little hops and barks in response, wagging his tail. My father repeats his game and Wolf barks more, lowers his head, and stands his ground, as if to attack. Then my father pats his head, first like affection, then harder, again and again. Wolf growls and returns to his position of attack. Things go on this way until Wolf grows up and my father decides the dog has to earn the bones he chews. My sister and I cry, but my father takes him to his shop of household appliances, where Wolf keeps guard on the patio. I miss him, and go play with him whenever I can, but he's more unfriendly every time. At some point he has to be tied up with a chain. The last time I go, he doesn't recognize me. To bring him water and food, the adults have to go out to the patio carrying a stick, on alert against the risk of attack. My father is the only exception. It's enough for him, unarmed, to bark at the dog while showing his teeth to make the beast to draw back, eyes shining and fur bristling, obedient though awaiting the slightest distraction to attack with a leap.

"Damned is he who cannot speak well of his own father" (John 1:3).

Like a dog. It occurs to me now that my father trained Wolf to attack just like his grandfather Salomón attacked Ernesto, my grandfather. I take it as a given that Ernesto received more blows from Salomón than he delivered to his son, and that my grandfather hit my father harder than my father hit me. Nor am I free of any guilt on those descending rungs. What I do know is that Ernesto lived an unhappy life. Instead of speaking, he grumbled. From my grandmother María, his wife, he received only displays of resentment and contempt. What I'm going to say now is something I initially wrote down for another family novel, but since the one who narrated the center of the story to me asked me not to publish it until after her death, those lines will be read here for the first time. Nearing eighty years old, my grandfather Ernesto began to suffer from a cancer of the stomach that he didn't want to treat. "What for?" he asked. "It's been long enough." With his cancer already progressing, he asked my grandmother María to cook the neck of a chicken and fill it with beef, onion, red bell pepper, and bulgur wheat, seasoned with pepper, salt, and grated baby radish. My grandmother told him it was going to upset his stomach, but he said to her: "You shut your trap now, and go make it for me." Conclusion, he ate that delicious piece of greasy meat, upset his stomach, felt bad and got into bed, and never got up again. When the family came to visit, he pointed at my grandmother and said: "She killed me." Of course, between the claim and the fact, several months went by. As he approached his end, a nurse tended to him, and for some reason I can't specify, maybe because of my status as an older grandson with "responsibilities," it was expected that I would spend my days at his house in Villa Lynch, witnessing his decline and keeping my grandmother María company. The nurse, whose name and appearance I don't remember, was a morbid woman, either cruel or devout, who recorded the ongoing cycle of events with clinical precision. One summer day, I got home early. My grandmother wasn't there; she'd gone to the shops. As soon as she saw me enter, the nurse told me to call my father and uncles, since my grandfather had at most an hour. I phoned the shop, of course, and as I did so, a wave of terrible hate overwhelmed me, far more powerful than any I'd felt before: Why did I have to be there, and not my father and uncles, the sons of the dying man? My grandfather had never loved me, or at least had never let me know it. Only once did he make a confession that expressed some humanity, or maybe just pity for himself. He said to me:

"Yes, I know I'm a brute, a beast, but don't you go thinking that your grandmother is a jewel. Just look at the things she says to me." Then I asked what she said to him, not because I wanted to know, but because it was the first time he'd acknowledged me as a conversation partner. He answered: "'Flea-bitten dog,' she says to me, 'when are you going to die?'" In exchange for that secret, which he could have kept quiet, I accompanied him through all his hospital admissions, starting at the German Hospital, which he entered shouting that the Nazis were going to kill him . . . I spent a night of Carnaval sleeping in a chair, when the only thing I wanted was to go out, and celebrate with my friends, and see the lights of life. Instead, just like always, I was there. I made calls, I let people know the situation, I asked them to come, and when I hung up my grandmother was opening the front door. She had a lost look in her eyes and barely seemed to recognize me. "How is he?" she asked. "Resting," I said. "No. He's at death's door," she said, and shut herself away in her own bedroom.

I entered my grandfather's room. He was breathing loudly, with eyes closed. The nurse touched his leg and said: "Can you feel your leg, Don Ernesto? Do you feel cold?" Then she moved her hand along his thigh, as she repeated the question. Death starts from below. My grandfather didn't answer: he was breathing with his mouth open, rumblings that lifted his chest for a second, then yanked it down like a collapse. At some point, the nurse told me: "Go outside, the worst is coming now, the rattles." I went out and waited. The door stayed open a crack. From the hall I could see nothing but a snippet of his arm, which moved a few centimeters, then stopped. Then the arm disappeared from the visual field, and

I saw only fragments of the body of the nurse, who had moved to the bed's headboard. A few minutes later, she left the room and said: "You can go in now." My grandfather wasn't moving. A handkerchief wrapped over his chin held the lower part of his jaw and pressed it against the upper part. The handkerchief was red and white with yellow dots, and the knot on his head gave him a vaguely feminine aspect, as if Ernesto had died after tying up his hair to clean the house. Over his closed eyelids the nurse had put two heavy silver coins, the national peso. I stayed looking at him and after a while began to cry, because in my way I had loved him, or at least hoped to love him. Ernesto, my grandfather, once bought three shirts in the same checkered design and same cut, and put one on, giving another to my father and the third to me. I was already his height and taller than my father, so the shirt fit me just right. When the three of us looked at ourselves in the dresser mirror, wearing our new shirts, I felt, maybe for the first time, a pride of belonging and sense of continuity. And now there he was, with his ridiculous little bow tie and those coins, so nobody would see the death in his dimmed eyes. While I was crying, my father came in, looked at me and said: "What are you doing here?" And I didn't answer, even though I could have said he knew very well why I was there, because he and his brothers didn't have the courage to accompany their dying father, and had delegated that task to me, with the excuse of having to keep busy with the family business.

But of course, no one can accompany a long agony without rest. Maybe they did everything they could to bear it. And in my father's case, maybe when he saw me before his father's corpse, he felt the need to protect me, even if it was too late, from the inevitable spectacle of death. Or maybe he wanted to remove me from the spectacle of his own pain.

I left the room.

———◆———

At a family lunch, I mention the scene with grandfather Ernesto to my uncle Alberto, and tell him that to this day I can't forgive the absence of his sons at the moment of his death. Alberto looks at me as if I were a stranger, a madman: "What are you saying? I was there. The nurse told me to leave the bedroom. I was there when my father was dying."

———◆———

After the last operation on my father's legs (acute arterial occlusion, with the placement of stents that became plugged within three months of surgery), he experienced effects with a complicated name, whose last word is *claudication*. Informally it's called "window-shopper's disease," because every half block, those affected can't take another step forward and must stop to rest. Just in case, foreseeing the advance of this illness, which in a severe case would include the amputation of one or both legs, a couple of months ago I got him a wheelchair that until yesterday he refused to try, for all I told him we could use it to move around the neighborhood. a couple of months ago I got him a wheelchair that until yesterday he refused to try, for all I told him we could use it to move around the neighborhood. On December 31st I had told his caretaker that before she went to celebrate the end of the year with her family, she should fold the wheelchair and load it in the taxi when she brought him to my home.

"Not that," he said to me, pointing to the chair with his index finger. He spent the whole afternoon sleeping, then I turned on the television and put on the nature documentary channel for him. All those who film the animal kingdom seem to adopt an identical narrative: an affectionate little beast, a herbivore, nibbles on grass or elegantly bends forward to take a drink of water from the stream, then suddenly we witness the predator's attack. After a couple hours of this repetition, he said he was tired. I took him to his room, helped him take off his clothes, drew back the sheet and blanket he needs to stay warm (he gets cold even when the temperature is over thirty degrees), and tucked him in. "Thank you, thank you," he murmured. "Call me if you need anything," I said. He asked me to bring him a Kleenex to blow his nose, then went to sleep. Some time later, fireworks began to sound in the sky, exploding sparklers. I went into the street to watch them and a neighbor invited me to drink a toast, but I told him my father was asleep at home and if he woke up and didn't see me, because of the disorientation in time and space, he'd suffer an episode of confusion. I returned home and climbed up to the terrace, but the sparklers and their cracklings of happiness were extinguished, and only the gleam of the city lights and the yellow of the moon could be seen. I stayed up there for just a short time, thinking that maybe he would wake up and not see me, and if he didn't see me he would miss me, because he does know who I am, even if at times he can't remember my name. But he rested for a solid twelve hours. Every so often I entered the bedroom to see if he was breathing, and every now and then he woke abruptly to use the toilet, dragging his feet like an old man who's just turned eighty-nine years old. After taking a piss he went back to bed, looking lost, and I went to the toilet and poured a mix of water and bleach into it and the area surrounding, because to aim, in his case, is no longer the same as to hit the target.

In the morning, while I prepared breakfast, he asked what we were doing at my house. "Nothing. We're going to play dominoes," I said. The game lasted for only a few minutes, because he kept confusing the value of the pieces and rubbing his hands against his temples. Then I said we were going to take a turn in his wheelchair. He refused. We walked for half a block before he had to stop. He massaged his calves at the height where they'd been cut open during the last operation. I sat on the edge of a low wall, in front of the barbed wire fence that borders the station. He likes to watch the arrivals and departures of the trains, and when he hears the noise of arrival I ask him where it comes from, and when the trains leave I ask him how many wagons each one has. There are six, every time, but he always counts them like he's never seen them before. This time he said, "Who knows," and I told him, "There are six," and he said, "And what do I know?" Then I told him to wait for me, I was going to look for the wheelchair and with the chair we could enter the station itself and count the wagons from up close. He stayed there, waiting, as I went home, walking slowly, stopping to tie the shoelaces of my trainers, thinking that each second of delay might produce an irreparable accident: that he would cross the street, or someone would mug him, or he'd get lost by himself, or simply vanish, but when I returned, he was in the same place where I'd left him. He sat down and I pushed the wheelchair uphill until we reached the station. I looked for a place in the shade and we stayed there watching the trains go by, not counting the wagons, just watching the people. To make sure the chair didn't move, I put the handbrake on. When the third train approached, I thought that maybe I could release the brake and push the wheelchair onto the tracks, at the exact moment the train passed.

When we got home, I asked him what he had thought of the outing. "Interesting," he said.

Sometimes, on Saturdays, we'd go have lunch at the home of my paternal grandparents. Ernesto and María lived in an old colonial house that had seen better days. They raised chickens in the back patio, where a reeking fig tree grew. My mother never went into the backyard for fear that the chickens would peck at the freckles on her arms, thinking they were grains of corn. Her only passion was fear. After eating, my father went to lie down in one of the rooms, and if I wanted to play for a while, kicking the ball against the walls, for example, my grandmother would forbid it, saying: "Your dad has to rest because he's nervous, he's sick. He isn't healthy like your grandpa."

For my mother, the word of her mother-in-law was holy writ. On Sunday afternoons at home, when my father wanted to rest, silence had to reign as in a provincial cemetery. It seems that I didn't follow the order of a deathly hush with the necessary rigor, and once, to ensure that his repose wouldn't be interrupted, my father even made me sleep in the matrimonial bed with him. A siesta is a necessity for babies and a habit for adults, but for a child, the obligation to keep still and silent is a torture.

The room is closed and retains the heat of summer. Sun strikes the wood shutters, and the half-closed lace curtains let through a bit of light. My father falls asleep immediately, and I stay watching the sun's glare on the door of the half-open wardrobe. A few silk or rayon ties hang from the rack, and the red and yellow and blue twinkle. I wait for him to enter into deeper dream, and as soon as his breathing slows I stretch out a leg and try to slip out of bed, to leave the room and head for the promise of the street. But he cracks open an eye and says: "Stay." I remain there a while longer, counting the seconds, which become minutes. "Sleep," he commands. I'm not sleepy, so I try to think of something, but nothing comes to mind except to measure the passing of time. The threads of light become more slender, losing intensity and growing faint, and slowly, the ties and the beveled mirror and the room begin to darken into shadow. I get up without making a sound and go into the yard, but my mother sees me and asks: "What are you doing here?" She raises a hand and points back toward the bedroom. Outside, the shining world is a story.

———◆———

The kitchen sink in his house gets blocked, a fluorescent tube stops working, the power switch for the patio light snaps. I head over with switches, starter, plunger, drain cleaners. After two hours of effort, it's clear that the drains need the inspection of a plumber, and I've only managed to confirm that he was right when he said I'm useless with practical matters. I resign myself to defeat, and leave everything in a worse state than I found it. We play dominoes for a while: the intention is for him to exercise his mind with calculations. It more or less works with sums, but he's already forgotten his multiplication tables. We go outside to walk his fifty steps. He drags his feet. The building next door is monitored by a private security guard. My father greets him with a salute, like a soldier. We come back inside and I tell him to water the garden. He does so for five, six minutes, then gets tired and sits down. I grab the hose, water the dry plants, and decide to test whether he can still guess my thoughts. I lift the hose, point it at the branches of the plants around him, then launch a brief jet in his direction for a second, not even a drizzle. He gives a start, and I laugh with the distressed cackle of a hyena. He smiles and opens a hand, as if he wants to say something but doesn't know what. "You were sleeping," I tell him. I can't explain how he's reached such a state of serenity. Maybe it's the cumulative effect of the psychotropic drugs, which he must take in industrial quantities to calm his anxiety and manage to sleep. I sit by his side. We look at the garden. "It's pretty," he says. We keep silent for a while. I move a hand along his back, I ask: "What's up with you, why aren't you talking?" He shrugs, and says: "The wet factory is closed." "The factory? Wet?" "Yes." When I get up to leave, I realize that I'm doing so because he wants me to go. He asks when I'll come back.

The Colombian woman who takes care of him during the week sends me five or six voice messages each day. Sometimes up to ten. "Good morning, Señor Daniel. How are you today? Very well I hope. I just wanted to tell you that last night your father didn't sleep at all, not at all, really, I couldn't rest for a second. He got out of bed every five minutes to use the toilet, and at three in the morning he started to get dressed, and when I went in to check on him he had on three T-shirts, and two dress shirts, and he told me it was time to go. 'But no, Don Luis!' I said to him. 'Go where? Where do you want to go at this time? Look what time it is.' Or he went to the kitchen and asked me to make breakfast. 'But Don Luis,' I said, 'we just had dinner! Go to sleep now, it's very late.' So he went and lay down and in five minutes he was going to the toilet again. That's how it was, I tell you, I hope you're very well today, have a magnificent day. Ba bay, thank you." "Hello, Señor Daniel. How are you? Very well I hope. So sorry to call again. I wanted to tell you that your father is being just awful, he told me to treat him very badly, and to hit him. Can you even imagine! 'No,' I said, 'how could I hit you, Don Luis?' But he said, 'Yes, hit me.' 'But no, Don Luis,' and he said, 'But yes.' And I'll tell you something else, but don't say I told you: I give your father the pills, the medicines, and if I leave them on a little plate on the table, he counts them first, one by one, then asks me what each is for, and if I turn around he tucks them in his pocket, or hides them in his mouth and later spits them out, or throws them out the window. One little thing, Don Luis . . . Don Daniel: in my room it's terribly hot and the fan only blows hot air and it's really miserable. Did you talk to the electrician to see when he'll install the capacitor for the air conditioner upstairs? Because the heat is terrible, I can't sleep, my head burns and I wake up soaked. Don't forget please to buy quince jelly for Don Luis, and the sweet little toasts that are so tasty and he likes so much. Ah and please, when you can, can you buy me a double bed? Because the bed I have is so tiny sometimes I wake up on the ground and the mattress is so sunk in you can't even rest, it's really bad for my back, my spine, no, I can't rest at all. Don't forget the medicines for your father: Midax, Omeprazol, Cilostazol, Tegretol, Sintrom, Alplax, Lexapro, Domperidona . . . Will the Coto card work to make the orders? Because the last time they came, they brought the whole order, then took it away because when they swiped the card, it said there were no funds. Also don't forget to buy those disposable elastic underpants, not the diapers, because he doesn't take them off right and goes on himself and gets all dirty. They have to be extra-large, wide waist." "Don Daniel, sorry to bother you again at this time, I know you asked me not to call you or send more than ten messages a day, but there's no water in the house, the neighbor came to see what's going on and there's no water in the tank, and I have to wash, what can I do? I can't stay like this, without water, just imagine . . . ! Can you come tomorrow, really early, to resolve the issue? Well, I won't bother you anymore, I hope you're very well, have a happy night and get some rest. Ba bay, thank you."

—•—

I pick up my father and take him to his podiatrist. Once a month, a toe of his foot gets infected, and the nail has to be removed, the wound cleaned, the pus removed. "Motherfucker, it hurts," he says. While the podiatrist does her job, I look for a painting teacher who can tutor him at home: painting is the last interest that remains to him, now that he doesn't even want to go into the garden and look at the plants, much less water them. His Majesty, the big, tyrannical child, has given way to the senior citizen, the benevolent and corporate way to refer to an old person. After I pick up him from the podiatrist, we walk for a few steps. His hand rests on my shoulder. "I have to tell you something. The nurse. She doesn't treat me right. All the time talking. Blah, blah, blah, blah," he says. "Dad. Women talk. What are you going to do. And this nurse may talk a lot, but she's a good person who takes care of you." "Blah. Blah. Blah. She never stops." "Yes, I know." "All day long with her little phone." "Yes. She's talking with her mother, who's an old lady and lives in Colombia." "Blah, blah, blah. She doesn't treat me right." "Does she yell at you? Does she hit you?" "I don't know what you mean. Blah. Blah. Blah. She treats me badly." "You said the same thing about all the nurses who took care of you before . . . Did they all treat you badly?" "Yes." "Does she cook for you?" "Yes. More or less. I don't know." "Does she bathe you?" "She talks a lot. And she's fat." "Are you angry with her?" "All day long, blah, blah, blah." "Are you angry because she told you that when you go to the toilet, you shouldn't force yourself, or stick in your finger to get anything out, because you hurt yourself?" "I don't know what you mean." "The doctor already told you not to do that, you hurt yourself with your nails and could get infected." "I don't know what you mean." "Listen to me, since all the señoras treat you so badly, what would you say if we took you to a place with little old men and little old ladies your age? Maybe you'll even find a new sweetheart." "Don't joke." "They'll give you tasty food . . ." "I really don't think they would." "Why not? Do you remember Grandma Rosa?" "Who?" "Doña Rosa, the mother of my mother, you went to visit her in the nursing home years ago. She did well there. She practiced gymnastics. She even found a new boyfriend." "Yes? How is she?" "She died." "Died?" "Yes, a long time ago." "I didn't know about that. She died?" "Yes. If she were alive now she'd be 130 years old. And Uncle Víctor and Aunt Noemí, Mom's siblings, they're dead too." "I didn't know any of that. And your mother?" "Don't you remember? You just saw her at home on Sunday." "Who?"

Víctor and Noemí, my mother's siblings. Víctor was a happy, simple man. Physically, he combined Elvis Presley in his decadence with Pocho La Pantera, adding to the version some forty kilos of his own style. He owned a sporting goods store in a rather bleak area of Villa Martelli, and when he got sick, his health insurance sent him to a public hospital in Pompeya. They informed us that he was dying, and we should come say goodbye. It was a struggle to convince my aunt Noemí, because her husband Arón was upset over some matter involving the division of family assets, but in the end we went. My uncle Víctor was in one of the beds in the intensive therapy sector, surrounded by other dying people, and by hospital norm we could only go in to visit him one at a time. His faithful wife Marta opened the door for us. After wiping away her tears, she mopped sweat from her husband's forehead using the same moist handkerchief. Noemí went in first, and came back five minutes later. We asked her how the goodbye went and what Víctor had said. "Marta said: 'Víctor, here's your sister Noemí,' and Víctor said: 'Noemí dear, I'm so happy you've come. I've always been very happy, everyone in the neighborhood loves me, I have no hard feelings toward anyone. Don Pancho the carpenter loves me, the greengrocer loves me, the neighbors love me. Everyone in the neighborhood loves me. I'm very content, I'm very happy, thank you for coming to see me.'" Then Arón went in, and to avoid digging up past differences he grabbed Víctor's hand and said: "Hello, Víctor, how are you?" Víctor repeated more or less the same phrases he'd said to Noemí, while Marta dried his forehead. Then I went in. His eyes were closed, and he'd removed his set of false teeth, and in his empty mouth there gleamed a single gold tooth. I imagine he chose that material at a lavish moment. Marta told him who'd come, she dried her tears with her handkerchief and passed it over Víctor's lips. And then Víctor said: "Dear," and started to repeat to me what he'd said before, like it was a prayer that would protect him from death and make him enter Paradise. Then, maybe because of the fever or painkillers, he started to rave. His monologue was rambling, and brilliant, I wish I'd had a recorder on me. At some point Víctor said goodbye and Marta told me to go get my mother, and my mother asked me to come in with her because she couldn't bear the thought of going in alone. Then I took her by the arm, and Marta dried the spittle on Víctor's lips and said to him: "Víctor, here's your sister Malvina, she's come to see you," and my mother said to him: "Hello, Víctor." And Víctor said: "Who are you?" My mother was surprised by the question and said: "It's me, I'm Malvina." And Víctor said: "Who's this? I don't recognize her." And you wouldn't believe my mother's anguish, she grabbed his hands and moaned: "Víctor, Víctor! I'm Malvina, your sister. Your older sister, Víctor. Don't you know me?" And Víctor started to laugh: "I know it's you, Malvina. It's only a joke."

That was Víctor. He was supposed to die that night, but he lasted five more years. Operations, hospital admissions. After the cancer occupied his intestine, he could eat only soft things. He asked for crustless ham and tomato sandwiches, like kids eat. He departed this world with a kiss of God on the forehead.

Just before she died, we went to visit Noemí at the clinic in

Coghlan where she'd been admitted. In her final moments, she confused people, times, and places, and asked my mother who was taking me to school. Her husband, Arón, wanted to know how my father was doing. I asked if he'd like to see him. "What I don't know is if you'll recognize him," I said. He thought about it, and said no. He preferred to remember him as he was before. "Your old man saved Noemí and me. When your grandfather died, your father took care of the money questions, because I was always useless in that area. If it weren't for him, we'd be bankrupt. I'm eternally grateful to your dad. He's truly a great person," he told me.

A short man, and a good man without knowing it himself, Arón was shaking when we said goodbye to Noemí amidst the mud of the open graves at San Martín cemetery. Sandra, Víctor's daughter, sang an ancient prayer for the dead, and Mom, hunched over in pain, suffocated by tears, spoke to the coffin as it descended: "Noemí, I know you're going to be somewhere with Víctor, soon the two of you will be sipping maté with those salty biscuits you liked so much."

She said that in a broken voice, my mother.

Many years ago, we went on vacation to a Japanese-themed park. I think we were spending the summer in Córdoba, because I vaguely recall some low mountains. But the memory might be false. A bull's-eye with the prize of a doll, a tent with an astrologer who read the future . . . One game drew my attention, maybe the most humble one there. On top of a table with a cotton cloth that reached to the ground, there was a white metal surface, with a red circle painted in the middle. The owner or manager of the game passed around three round white bottle caps, which we placed in the circle. The diameter of the caps averaged two-thirds the diameter of the circle, so that distributed in the correct manner, they could easily be arranged to cover it completely. The game, the seductive proposal of the game, was to imitate the movements of the manager and set the bottle caps on the red circle until it was covered. I don't remember the prize, but I do remember that when my turn came to play, I tried to cover the circle by putting down the first and second bottle caps, then the third. But when I tried, there was something like a layer of air or resistance that served as a cushion between the caps already placed, loosening them so they wouldn't fit. The third bottle cap shifted so a half-moon of color remained visible, a fingernail clipping, the naked red proof of my failure. I tried two, three times in a row. Impossible. Then I gave up, or my parents decided I'd spent enough.

Of course it isn't that I calculated badly or my pulse shook, or that my clumsiness was greater than the average player's. Hidden under the tablecloth there must have been a system of gears and interrupters that operated a magnetic device, worked by a pedal. The manager could connect or disconnect it at will: disconnect it when he put down the three caps, and reconnect it at the moment the player put down the second or third cap. The magnetism produced its attraction or repulsion, pushing the remaining bottle cap from its axis, so it covered the diameter in an imperfect way. The curious thing is that my failure at this game, in appearance so simple, devastated me. The red circle was a threat I had to cover up but that insisted on showing itself, and the reiterated attempts transformed it into a proliferating monstrosity impossible to combat. Yet the consequence is that in the long term, this produced a lesson, or rather became a decision: since then I haven't been able to take an interest in artworks (books, music, paintings, sculptures) that wager everything on the perfect, the complete and closed. I want to keep on seeing the red, what cannot be covered, not necessarily a circle but a circuit of repetition and persistence, the mark of error. What's more, and in another order of things, this experience was linked to a design that might be considered random, but for me is central: a rectangle with a red circle painted in the middle. The design of the Japanese flag: a red solar disc on a white background. Another source of my obsession with the oriental, perhaps. The eye fixates on something that must be concealed or revealed, as in the case of the little Chinaman at the bottom of the plate of soup. And returning to that subject, now I understand the hidden reason that motivated the intervention of my paternal grandmother, who interrupted the pediatrician's absurd cure with her spoonfuls of honey. After the birth of my sister, my mother lived for a few months submerged in postpartum depression. I don't retain the slightest image of it. In my first memories of childhood, she appears as a gypsy with curly red hair, and huge shiny gold hoops dangling from her ears. But it's more probable that in this period she spent hours and days and weeks lying in bed, with barely enough strength to breastfeed my sister, maybe without the energy to feed herself well either. From which I deduce that my own lack of hunger, my convulsive gestures of protest, imitated those of my baby sister Chuchi as she came away from the breast, frustrated by the small amount of milk she could consume; and even more importantly, my hunger strike demonstrated a kind of essential solidarity with my mother. Over the course of these pages, I've painted her in the colors of thoughtlessness, cruelty, and egoism, but only now can I understand that things were not the way I've been telling them, just as only now can I understand how very linked I was to her, how very much I loved her and pitied her fate, to the point that I chose to die with her, or die for her, if such a thing ever became necessary.

———◆———

When my father was a child, he accompanied my grandfather Ernesto to his work as a porter at the Israelite Hospital. As soon as they got there, he headed for the elevator and earned a few coins by pressing buttons, as he picked up and dropped off people at their floor. As a young man he liked to tango and cultivated the fine moustaches of the singers in fashion. As soon as he could, he began to earn money playing roulette at the casino and bought shares on the stock market, falling in platonic love with women of an intellectual air (my sixth-grade teacher, a television news anchor). He wanted to start a revolution but couldn't put up with the dogmatism of the Party, he was generous with friends and happy outside the home, he told me that money didn't matter and I had to concern myself with what interested me. And now he opens his wallet in silence for me to slip hundred-peso notes inside, rejecting those of lesser value since "they aren't interesting, they aren't important." What can one say about a father?

My mother was always terrified of poverty, police persecution, and animals. When she was a girl, a dog barked at her and in her panic she fell into a hole my grandfather had dug for a septic tank. At night she couldn't sleep listening to the neighing of a horse or the wingbeats of bats. When she was even younger and her sister Noemí was just a few months old, the drinking water in the area became contaminated and gave Noemí diarrhea, and when my grandparents went to check her into hospital my mother stayed with the neighbors and suffered, thinking her parents had abandoned her. Now she cultivates her passion for discovering new medical problems, and sings in a choir, her face radiating happiness. Like it does when she talks with her grandchildren or talks about them. She visits the rabbi, collects saint cards, and has a manual of Buddhist prayers in Sanskrit with syllabic translations in Spanish, whose mantras she repeats when nervous. She says that separating from my father was the best thing she did in life, but every time we speak on the phone she asks after his health. What can one say about a mother?

A Chinese communist leader once said that in the final instance, existence determines consciousness.

As soon as our economic situation improved, my mother decided to incorporate some habits of social ascent. She began to take English classes, in anticipation of future trips abroad (which my father's second wife would enjoy). Along with a group of friends, she also signed up for ikebana lessons with Señora Tazuko Nimura in the Villa Devoto neighborhood. She soon developed a great passion for the subject, which spread to the family circle: on each outing to the countryside, beach, park, or mountain, my father would stop the car on the side of the road, and my sister and I would get out to collect branches, flowers, reeds, and anything else of a reasonable size, with the idea that once back home, she'd insert fine wires into each stalk to achieve the artificial twistings that are the most elevated dimension of the aesthetic will. In those moments, we worked as a single organism, making common cause with that activity of my mother, who at those moments seemed to be, or transformed into, another person, bolder, more restless, more determined. I remember her contemplating our harvests with a critical eye, gently shaking a flower in the air to test its capacity for torque, the angle of its turn. We felt happy when we set down those offerings from the excursion on the table, and at some point (I imagine more than remember it) we shuddered to see how green sap spurted from the ends of each cut branch as the needles of the prongs pierced into their interiors. Mother jammed them in with force, sinking the iron tips in deep, and the flesh felt the pain. Then, with each vegetal piece fixed, she began to give them form, indicating to nature the necessity for it to submit to the mandates of art. The idea of a miracle, which comes from irrational faith, is ultimately secondary to the phenomenon of the transformation of nature by civilization, which is why nobody truly believes in gods but everybody, at some point, has felt the beneficial effects of the cultural practice of prayer. So the family waited in reverence for the conversion of those humble branches and tiny stalks into beautiful pieces that would ignite hope in a greater destiny. With her floral art, my mother, the subjected and fearful one, the informer, illuminated our lives.

Of course we were also hoping her works would take top prize in the annual competition organized by the Ikenobo Society of Ikebana Art. Unfortunately, though she submitted to contest after contest, nobody saw as clearly as we did the real dimension of her achievements, their genuine beauty. Time after time she obtained a first, second, or third mention, in a descending scale that followed after the first, second, third, fourth, and sometimes fifth prizes.

In any case, she didn't lose heart. During the award ceremonies she gave thanks, bowing her head like a true Japanese woman and lifting her hands up to receive the diploma scroll tied with red silk ribbon, while others, even her own friends, received a cup, medal, or trophy. My mother didn't surrender before the modesty of those results, didn't rebel at their injustice. Ikebana was an aesthetic that led to an ethic of personal transformation.

The change was external, too. Each ikebanist transformed herself into an example of the art that she practiced. This involved weekly visits to the hairdresser (it was the age of stiff high updos, fixed in place by a shiny hair spray net), the constant acquisition of dresses and shoes, and meetings at the houses of her workshop colleagues to debate the tradition and renovation of floral arrangement, secret queens of the suburb. All this, plus the time she dedicated to her English classes, meant she had to leave our house for a few hours each day, leaving me in the company of the maid.

If I'm truly embarrassed to confess anything, it's this: every time my mother headed for the door, ready to go out—with her complex architecture of perfectly assembled hair, her tight polyester silk dress just barely covering her knees, her sunglasses with pointy corners and fake diamonds at the arch, her shoes with stiletto heels that tapped against a floor made of similar spruce wood, and her imitation crocodile leather purse dangling from her arm—I spread open my arms, pinned myself to the door, and started to whimper: "No, don't leave me, don't go!"

Since this was a daily scene, the sequence of events quickly developed a pattern: from the initial persuasion, the sweet voice trying to convince her darling that mommy would come back very soon, she passed to an impatient tone, then to exasperation, before finally she made a gesture to the maid, who picked me up in her arms and removed the obstacle of my presence, as my mother disappeared into the light of the outside world.

I remained there shaking, agitated, crying with rage. In my egoism, I didn't even allow myself to consider that those outings were required by her dedication to the cause of ike-bana, and that in her way she was fighting for and seeking to obtain supremacy in her art, just as we all hope to do. At those moments, with the greed of abandonment, I began to count the minutes that separated her absence from the fulfill-ment of her promise of return, also considering the possibility that the outing would be definitive. The horrifying idea of that possibility plunged me into phantasmagorias of melan-choly, the product of reading horror stories (about children who had been orphaned, starved, ridiculed, abandoned, mar-tyred, sacrificed, abused, shot, murdered). I passed the time in such entertainments, and all at once surprised myself with the discovery that the tragic sense of life had passed, and I man-aged quite well in solitude.

This glimmer of independence, however, was darkened by the identical discovery that my mother was also capable of a life independent from me. And thus I existed in the cradle of the hours, rocking between resentment and oblivion. At some point, the sound of the key inserting itself in the lock of the door could be heard. Then I lowered my head, seized by an emotion of revenge, and pretended to concentrate on my game (figurines, marbles, Meccano), while really thinking: "So you came back . . . You couldn't live without me. Me."

———— ◆ ————

A Jewish joke that isn't one.

At the first performance of a theatrical work, my mother—who for twenty years studied theater as a hobby—bumps into a Jewish-Argentine writer, a pro-government professional the international press has called the "Woody Allen of the Pampas." She, who only knows him from photos, goes up and says:

"Are you XXX?"

"Yes, Señora," he says, swelling with pride for being recognized.

"Ah, good. I'm the mother of . . ." she says, and names me, swelling with pride herself for making me known.

Another:

Sunday lunch, with family. Pasta.

Her: "Why are YYY and ZZZ translated in France, and not you?"

Me (*irritated, bleeding from the wound that she reopens*): "Mom, can you let me eat lunch in peace?"

Her: "Well, I'm only saying so for your sake. I don't know why someone doesn't see to it."

———— ◆ ————

The abomination of waste. If at dinner I left a bit of the stringy, semi-raw meat stuck to the rib on my plate, my father would say: "Marx and Engels would have finished the steak, because they knew the value of money and food." Or he'd nationalize the example by using a deliveryman for the family business as his model, and say that in my place, the workman would have grabbed the bone with his fingers and sucked at it until the rib was shiny clean, because those guys knew the true meaning of hunger.

His system was grounded in the idea of starting at the bottom, in a daily job, to forge a base in the culture of effort. And so, during summer vacations when all of my friends were spending the days playing football in the street, or soaking up the sun, or swimming in pools at suburban clubs, I had to go to work as an office boy at our branch facing the Plaza San Martín. I had the same schedule as all the other employees, from eight thirty in the morning to seven in the afternoon, with two hours free for lunch and a period of rest on the fake leather sofas in the administrative sector. It was assumed that through years of physical activity, I would end up learning the secrets of the business, perhaps by osmosis. The family business was a mini-chain, the Refrigerator Supermarket: the owners were my father and two uncles, David and Alberto. Central headquarters were in the Once neighborhood, but my father was in charge of the store in San Martín, the neighborhood where we lived.

At eight thirty in the morning, I would enter that huge awful storehouse and confront the silent rows of refrigerators with an emptiness in my soul. I never counted them, but there must have been one or two hundred, all white, smelling of the foul dead material of sheet metal, painted with a blowtorch. The pride of my father and uncles, that special something which defined them as businessmen dedicated to the greater cause of client satisfaction, was what they referred to as "exclusive pre-delivery service." It meant, first of all, that before organizing the weekly distribution of sold merchandise, every item was plugged into an electrical outlet and tested for twenty-four hours to guarantee correct functioning, a requirement not violated even when a rushed buyer wanted to take the refrigerator home that very moment. Second, and most important, the electrical appliance was delivered in a state of absolute cleanliness, as if the company were incarnating the lyrics of the Chilean singer Antonio Prieto: "White and radiant goes the bride . . ." The one in charge of delivering the goods this way, in a condition of impeccable purity, was me. Supplied with a bucket of water, soap, and a rag, I'd rush to the exit where deliveries left from to remove the tiny mud stains that clung to the outsides of each refrigerator, double check the weather strips, and wipe down the racks, shelves, and egg boxes. This operation of excellence was the final maestro's flourish of another that preceded it, and needed to be carried out with regularity: the passing of a feather duster over the upper part, let's call it the roof, of the refrigerator, because it was where dust in the air tended to gather.

As soon as I entered the store, I started in on that task, and after an hour and a half, each of the refrigerators had been feather dusted. Of course any person with a minimum of intelligence knows that the basic function of a duster is to shift dust from one place to another. And so to prevent dusted material on the top part of the refrigerator from floating, gently or violently, until it settled on the top of its neighbor (to one side of it, or in front of or behind it), I'd developed a technique that began with a horizontal sweep over the surface toward the four edges, before with a flick of the wrist, I performed a vertically descending movement that forced the dust, in theory, to fall to the ground. Well then. I carried out this task with the ability that weeks of practice give. Refrigerator after refrigerator, surface after surface, wrist flick after wrist flick. At around ten or ten thirty in the morning, my father made his appearance on the premises. All of my efforts collapsed at that moment. He would lift his index finger, and on his way toward the back of the storehouse where the managers' office was located, slide it over the top of each refrigerator, one after another. He'd walk as if he hadn't seen me, without even greeting me, as his examining index finger dedicated a caress to each electrical appliance. But such affection was mere appearance, for it was really a test. When he reached the final refrigerator in the row he delayed for a while longer, as if wanting to compensate with frosty silence the ardent knowledge he was withholding, then he turned back to me, showing me his finger: on its tip one could see what his round of inspection had gathered and could not be eradicated, the ashen mark of my failure: dust.

Then I had to go sweep the feather duster again.

Witnessing the repetition of this scene, a seller in the storehouse once approached me: "Why are you doing that?" she asked.

"If I don't sweep, dust will gather."

"It's going to gather anyway, the refrigerators have a static electricity that condenses it."

"You mean the dust floating in the atmosphere is attracted . . ."

"Obviously. Every refrigerator works as a kind of magnet . . ."

"And so?"

"So what?"

"Does that mean I don't have to listen to my old man?"

"The result will be the same, whatever you do."

"So I can do anything?"

"You could."

"But what should I do?"

"If you choose to clean, you are complying with your father's order. But your compliance is not definitive and total, since you know the outcome is destined to failure. Therefore your compliance possesses in its interior a noncompliance, given that although you are doing what you are doing, you are aware you are not achieving the desired result. At the same time, if you choose not to clean, disobeying his order, the result is also noncompliance, with disobedience affecting not the consequence, but the nature of the link with your father."

"Then what do I need to do?"

"How can you expect an employee to give you an objective answer? If I encouraged you in the sentiment of rebellion, I'd put my job, monthly salary, and the nourishment of my children at stake. Therefore, in the defense of my interests, I beg you to continue following orders and sweeping the feather duster until you lose consciousness, until in the vertigo of your task you forget your vexatious insistence on meaning, until you are absorbed by the senselessness of your aim."

"But does my father know that the static captures the dust I clean, and makes it come back to the dusted surface? Is it the same dust, or similar but different dust, floating in the atmosphere . . . ?"

"He knows and always has known, in advance of his giving you the task. How could he not have known, if he studied electricity and is a specialist in refrigeration?"

"Then why . . . ?"

"Why don't you ask him?"

I went to the managers' office. A frosted glass door with an inscription in black letters said: "Knock before entering." I obeyed, as always. Three knocks on the glass. Fewer might not be noticed; more would be an abuse. From the other side, my father's voice: "Come in."

"What do you need?" he asked when he saw me. It was his usual question and couldn't be answered, since the word "need" always seems to be linked to the criterion of truth, and none of what I wanted to say could be encompassed by the purely communicational intention of his statement. What I needed was something that could not be spoken, something whose identity even I didn't know. But now I was filled with rage, maybe the same kind that Wolf felt as he walked around, back and forth, in the yard, across the patio, rattling his dragging chain. Yes, I was filled with rage, and now I was no longer a kid, and rage led me to believe that I could confront him, because by that stage, as he himself had said, we were able to speak like two adults.

"I'm not going to feather dust refrigerators anymore," I said to him. My father had been smiling. He was sitting, or rather reclining, on his ergonomic leather sofa. But when he heard my phrase, he sat upright and leaned his elbows on the table and his head into his hands.

"No? And why not? Maybe you think that we should give clients dirty merchandise?"

"Because it's a useless job."

"Useless?"

"Yes."

"And why useless?"

"Why are you asking me like you don't know the answer?"

"Because I can't believe what you're telling me. What does it mean that you aren't going to feather dust my refrigerators anymore, because it's a useless job? Do you think that the refrigerators will feather dust themselves?"

"I'm not saying that I think they clean themselves, I'm saying that now you realize I know it's a useless job. And you've always known and have hidden it from me, forcing me to do it just because, for no reason. To mess around with me, like always. You and your jokes. With the refrigerators and their static electricity . . ."

"What are you talking about? The refrigerators don't have static electricity."

"What do you mean they don't?"

"No. They're made of sheet metal. Only plastic has static electricity."

"So why does your finger . . ."

"Because you never clean well, because nothing is ever clean enough in this world and something never comes from nothing. What do you suppose is going to happen when I'm older and your uncles are older and we can't continue at the head of the business? You have to learn a sense of discipline. Or do you think a revolution happens just like that, from one day to the next, because you want it to, spontaneously? The same is true for your business, your heritage: the business is something, not nothing. Something we built with our efforts, saving peso by peso. At your age I was already working as a weaver at a factory in Villa

Lynch. The sound of the wool shuttles, coming and going, split open your brain. And I did three full shifts, one after another, after I married your mother. To bring home the bacon. When we were kids, your uncles and I got the poor man's coupon book the government distributed. With that booklet we could have school supplies delivered. We were always hungry. It's something you have to imagine, because you can't understand. A stable job saves you from hunger. If you work for hours and hours, without thinking, it's all profit, because the time passed is time that earns you money to buy food. If you'd known from the start that your job was useless, you wouldn't have learned a thing."

"And now what have I learned? Electromagnetism?"

"No," said my father, detecting a note of mockery and looking at me like he'd never seen me before. "Do you remember how a few years ago, when you and your sister were kids, I'd read you stories at night?"

"I don't remember."

"You don't remember because you don't want to remember. Every day after dinner, you and your sister brushed your teeth and lay down in your beds, and I came to the room with a book. Then I sat down on a chair and started to read to you. You, especially, had been waiting all day long for that moment, and while we were eating you wouldn't stop asking: 'What are you going to read us today, Daddy?' And even though I wanted to calm your anxiety by giving you a hint of what was to come, I knew that in the delay, the reserve, a deeper and wider plea-sure was hidden than any immediate reply would have given. So I answered you: 'Mystery.' Then you asked: 'Is it going to be a mystery story?' And I said: 'It might be mystery, terror, adventure, romance. What do you like most?'"

"And what did I say?"

"Nothing. I knew your favorites were terror, the infinite adventure of mental suffering embroidered in fantasies and words. But being the way you are, you preferred to shake your frowning little head before you'd admit to it. So I said: 'Wait and see.' And we ate our meal as a joyful family, and at the end your mother served us one of those tasty desserts she always made, and after brushing your teeth, you and your sister ran to bed waiting for the happy moment of the story that opens the doors to dream. And I began to read. My voice, I now know, produced a calming effect, because your sister fell asleep right away. You, on the other hand, resisted, though on more than one occasion you didn't make it to the end either. I'd give up my remaining years of life to go back to those times . . . Once . . . on one occasion . . . I read one whose title I still remember, 'The Little Florentine Scribe,' but I can't recall the name of the author. It's the story of an Italian family, poor, very poor. The father works for an office, a law firm, something like that. He does something that doesn't exist anymore, he's a copyist. He copies manuscripts, envelopes, I don't remember what now either. Maybe for his law firm. Legal language, boring. Trials, lawsuits, seizures, claims, expropriations, appeals, legacies, wills, inheritances. Day after day, the father dips his pen into the inkwell, copies out the lawsuit, absorbs the excesses of ink with blotting paper . . . And the same at home. He puts in extra hours at night, so there's bread on the table for his family. So many envelopes or pages, so much money. The world of conflicts and conciliations between parties scrolls before his eyes, and if the man wanted to, he could have learned the horrors and joys of others. But he copies automatically now, without thinking. That could indicate a greater efficiency acquired over the course of years, an automation that results in a superior quickness. But lately his rhythm has slowed. The father is old, his body no longer tolerates this work paid by the job. His fingers suffer from the effects of osteoarthritis, and constant inclination over the table produces a contraction of muscles and shifting of bones in the spine, with their resulting pains: a humpback, pinched vertebrae, a crushed lumbar spine. For all the efforts he makes, the ration of food grows leaner each week. One night after he goes to sleep, exhausted, his male son, the firstborn, conscious of the paternal deterioration, without letting him know and in silence, decides to continue the task. The son is clever, he knows how to imitate his father's handwriting; he's a good copyist of the copyist. The father has left a word, half-written: 'Req.' He completes it: 'Request.' And he continues until dawn, copying page after page. When his father gets up in the morning, he's astonished by the advance of the task, and comments on this at the table over breakfast, dry bread from the previous day, water. He says: 'Last night I worked very well. With what they pay me, I'll be able to buy half a dozen eggs. We'll dine on omelets. And there'll be enough for half a loaf of bread.' On the pale, ashen face of the mother, a smile appears. The son, the firstborn, also smiles, but to himself, and pledges to continue with his secret mission: to help his father and alleviate the family's economic situation. So each night, after his exhausted father lies down to sleep, he gets up in silence, goes barefoot from his bedroom to the kitchen where his father works, dips the pen into the inkwell, and copies out the previous handwriting, envelope after envelope, page after page. This lasts for days, maybe weeks. But he also has to go to school, and as his fatigue accumulates, his output begins to decrease. His father, who is unaware of his son's activity at night, receives the school bulletin and sees that the grades are going down, and that his firstborn in whom he'd placed all his hopes is becoming a bad student. Finally he confronts him, and makes his disappointment known through harsh words. The son, instead of replying, bites his lips until they bleed: he must not express the nature of the sacrifice, because to reveal it would imply the moral breakdown of his father, who would understand that he is no longer capable of maintaining his family. The father sees his son's grimace, the paleness of his lips and the sudden trickle of red liquid, and interprets his gestures as a display of pride. So he raises his voice and accuses him of being lazy, idle, good-for-nothing. Piercing through the quiet of the city, or its usual bustle, the sudden tumult of a cry of innocence can be heard, and now there is nobody or nothing who understands, for the shout has become double. The angels also shout in the heavens, clamoring against the injustice, but God, who dwells in the time of eternity, turns a deaf ear: he is studying. In the meantime, the mother twists her hands in desperation. Behind the father, the mother. What does the son do after that scene? Does he desist? Does he attempt to recuperate his father's affection by improving his performance at school in exchange for an abandonment of the secret task? No. His personal salvation would imply the family's ruin. So he redoubles his efforts, he copies and copies until dawn arrives, then he gets dressed, making no noise, and goes to school without rest. He sacrifices himself so much, and so fully, that one of those many nights while writing, out of pure fatigue, he falls asleep. His body slackens, and he collapses on the table with such bad luck, that his left elbow involuntarily knocks against a book of synonyms on the edge of the table. The book falls to the floor and the son immediately wakes, terrified by the possibility that his secret will be revealed. But the house remains in silence. The son picks up the book after a few seconds, stealthily, and goes on writing, concentrating on his task without realizing that his father, hearing the sound, has got up and just as stealthily gone to the kitchen, and is seeing now for the first time, with eyes blurred by tears, the truth. Then the father goes and kneels before his son, embraces him and begs his forgiveness, and kisses his hands. Are you crying?"

"Yes, Dad," I say, and I understand something that is my salvation, or my ruin: if I'd done something of the dimension that opens this story, then my father and I would be in the same situation, and our happiness complete. Whereas I, like a child, had complained about having to feather dust refrigerators . . . The comprehension of this descends upon me like a hammer blow from the abyss. I raise my head and say:

"Thank you, Dad, for awakening my love of literature."

At some point in the Jewish diaspora's thousands of years of history, a method arose to interpret the precepts of the Talmud. This method was called pilpul, which in Hebrew simultaneously means "pepper" and "sharp analysis," that is, spicy thought, and which expresses the will to achieve, through logical operations and the oppositions of reasonings, the infallible and unique sense of Jehovah's message. It is at once a corroboration of the imperfection of human thought and an examination of the nooks and crannies of the divine mind, which reveals a secret distrust in its judgment and harbors a secret suspicion: that God is mad. It's clear that this work of mental hygiene was not picked up by the younger Christian brothers, who by the second century were already convinced that the less comprehensible the dogmas of their new religion were, the greater the conviction needed to support them. In *De carne Christi*, Tertullian affirms this in a paradoxical and beautiful way.

> *The Son of God was crucified: there is no shame in this,*
>   *for it is shameful.*
> *And the Son of God died: by all means to be believed,*
>   *since it is absurd.*
> *And buried, He rose again: a certainty,*
>   *because it is impossible.*

In summary, the fundamental act of knowledge is an act of faith, and through intellectual surrender, by bringing the mind to its knees, our species is asking for divine help to achieve certainty regarding the ultimate end of all things. Saint Augustine gives some nuance to the statement "I believe because it is absurd," by affirming: "I believe to understand." Which would mean that the work of God is beyond the reach of human reason, or that to achieve understanding, a prior renunciation of the powers of thought is necessary.

Evidently, this was not the perspective that allowed for the development of pilpul. The method was first invented (or discovered) by Rabbi Jacob Pollak, who applied it to a case of family divorce over the division of goods, then extended its use to the collective body of Jewish religious precepts, derived from the written and oral Torah, whose interpretation parted the waters between different rabbinical schools. Pollak's method mainly consisted of a sort of mental gymnastics that allowed one to trace the relations between divergent and even contradictory ideas, propose questions, and resolve them in unexpected ways. In fact, its primary function was to keep students at the yeshiva awake. After his death in 1541, Pollak's main disciple Shalom Shachna broadened the perspectives of the method and established the bases for its use as they are known (or disregarded) to this day. Of course, save through the art of anachronism, neither Pollak nor Shachna was aware of the phrase that defines theology as a discipline without object, yet it was precisely the elusiveness of the presence of God, the contradictory nature of His operations, and the necessity of finding a general meaning in His work (and His existence) that drove them to elaborate a form of thinking that they believed could trap Him. For the infinite and uncapturable presence, the infinite nets of the word were necessary.

The mind, like the sea, the mind, the mind
that always begins again!
After a thought, what sweet recompense
to look at length upon the divine unrest!

To pursue Jehovah, to snare Him in contradictions, to cast the blame on Him for the imperfection and absurdity of His creation: that was the true mission of every good Jew. Devotion is a mask that conceals the irreverent suspicion that He is a joke. Instead of playing a game of chess against Him to vanquish His messenger Death, the pilpulist suspends time in the eternity of the reflexive act.

Pilpul was used to thoroughly analyze each part of the subject under consideration. One could take any sentence from the Torah, for instance, clarifying the correct sense of each term, letter, and space between letters, and then return that sentence to its original place, its rationality having been demonstrated. Its analysis complete, the sentence was then examined in relation to its historical, cultural, and semantic context, and if one discovered that analysis of the particular did not coincide with the situation or general field, one took up the task anew.

Now then, though the preceding example is simple enough stated thus, it is obvious this system of verification is long, arduous, and complicated, and nothing guarantees a general agreement of parts in the final result. Even so, it is nothing compared to the deployment of resources necessary when the topic under discussion becomes more complex. To penetrate into the essence of a subject and adopt clear distinctions and a strict differentiation of related concepts also implies the anticipation, or at least careful investigation, of the possible consequences that might be implied by such differentiation. If, for example, from two sentences that agree or are even identical, two pilpulists were to draw contradictory conclusions, signaling that the apparent coincidence did not in fact point to agreement, then the pilpulistic method would have to determine whether this apparent contradiction could not be eliminated through a series of more careful definitions and more exact delimitations of the concepts associated with the respective sentences. In the same way, if two adjacent sentences seem to possess the same meaning, the method would have to determine if the second sentence is a simple repetition of the first that could have been omitted, or if through a more subtle scrutiny of concepts, one could perceive a difference of degree in the meanings of each one. And even should one arrive at a positive result with the object of investigation (phrase, maxim, fact, precept, narration, law, saying, custom, history, parable, or legend), the practitioner of pilpul would have to ask himself if he could not have arrived at this same result in another way, supporting his conclusions based on a different system of proofs, in the event that the first procedure were refuted.

Pilpul expanded quickly through several countries (Lithuania, Poland, Ukraine), and a good part of the Jewish community soon developed a passion for following the scholars capable of working critically and obsessively on any topic. Bands of fanatics were set up in favor of this or that rabbi, the plazas of ghettos became forums of discussion, and good Jews entertained themselves with argument for hours, to the point of leaving aside games like chess and dominoes. To promote the activity, it was exaggeratedly claimed that Yahweh himself sometimes came down incarnated as a common Jew and participated in the discussions, losing on the majority of occasions. It was also even said in a low voice (these were times when anti-Semitism flourished) that Jesus (Yeshu, Jehoshua) had practiced the rudiments of pilpul but had not demonstrated great talent in the exercise.

After the flourishing came a fatal decadence. In his painful old age, Shalom Shachna saw how the axe of internal critique fell upon pilpul: the traditionalists accused those sparks of maniacal logic of belonging to the field of sophistry, and serving more as an exhibition of vain intelligence than as an investigation of truth. Pilpul entered into a cone of shadow that would last for several centuries, and the darkness spread, beginning with those who had promoted it. In fact, only one of Shachna's treatises was published, the indispensable *Pesachim be-Inyan Kiddushin*. Perhaps this is due to the fact that the wise man was a paragon of modesty, and on his deathbed he authorized his son Israel to print any one of his manuscripts, or better yet, not print any of them. In all of this, more than the echo, one finds the source itself of the literary activity of Franz Kafka, and his final decision, plea, or order given to Max Brod to burn his work. Kafka is the final exponent of pilpul and the one who has enabled its most far-reaching diffusion. Going further: those rhetorical operations at the end of the Middle Ages, rescued and processed in literary language by the little Jew from Prague, are the form chosen by the twentieth century to understand itself. The casuistic language; the hierarchies as a form of the infinite; the deferral; the patient and resigned approach to the impossible; the intractable machine of the real that resolves itself in the senselessness of every paradox, rendering the meaning of existence unreal: all of this as much prefigures the horror of the concentration camps (a claim often made) as it recuperates the opacity of a construction that pretends to lose its way, enchanted by the possibility of revelation, only to become entangled in the evidence that no genuine resolution exists. Of course, Kafka is a pilpulist so extreme that he seems a heretic to the tradition he takes up and rewrites. While the wise Jewish pilpulists are inconsistent with their own method because they believe their task is limited to the examination of the Revelation which Moses received from God—an examination that would conclude by arriving at an indisputable, all-encompassing truth derived from the combative nature of interpretations—for Kafka, in contrast, the Law is no longer God but the Father, and the struggle is no longer to understand

Him (for the Father, like God, is at the mercy of His own whim, and of the violence of His formulations) but to be understood by Him, and to confront Him in order to survive.

———— ◆ ————

When he was happy, my father sang tangos. Often at night I too secretly lit the lamp on my bedside table, turned on the Wincofón record player and listened at low volume to two albums with the greatest hits of Julio Sosa and Carlos Gardel. Stories of abandonment, turf, problematic loves, nostalgias in exile, competitions between men, deceitful women and infidelities, regrets, betrayals. By then I was already aware of the local myth that affirmed there has never been nor ever will be a singer superior to Gardel, the "singing bronze." But for all that I liked his songs, there was something in his nasal drawl and the sound of his *erre*, a certain chirping, high-pitched element, that to my young ears didn't sound completely virile. My favorite was Sosa, the real man of tango. While my father was sleeping, I secretly identified with his tastes, and put in my extra hours as a little Argentine listener playing his tangos, to feel I was a man like him. During that period Sosa died in a car accident, and it surprised me to hear the story that when undressing his corpse to swap out the items of clothing for the final ones that would accompany him in the coffin, the funeral home employees found he was wearing, instead of boxers, pink ladies' panties. Surely this anecdote is false, an invention by the band of fanatical Gardelians to diminish the image of their rival.

In any case, going back to the question of identification with the "true voice of a man": I remember that once, my father and

I were driving in his car, a vehicle with a radio always tuned
to a frequency that played music from the outer suburbs of
Buenos Aires. This time we were listening to a singer with a
drawling voice, a professional porteño who scanned his sylla-
bles like a German barbarian trying to decipher the structure
of Latin. His intonation rarefied the atmosphere as we passed
in silence through some lost corner of those suburbs. My father
had asked me to accompany him to visit a refrigerator manu-
facturer, and on the way back from the excursion, tedious and
full of speculations about the economic growth of the country,
he attempted to initiate a broader dialogue, moving from adult
to preadolescent territory, which included the topic of my
future sex life. But once the necessary prolegomena had been
discussed (preventive medicine, risks, desired and undesired
pregnancies), perhaps spurred by the memory of his youth,
perhaps by the desire to get closer to me by communicating
something of his experience, he mentioned a teenage girlfriend. For him, to name her was to relive the experience. He
said this woman had been his great love, that he had lost her
due to a misunderstanding. The malice of their parents, a dark
design . . . A silence fell, both of us contemplating the succes-
sive ugliness of the neighborhoods we passed through, and then
suddenly, giving a sharp blow to the wheel, he told me you have
to choose who you marry with the greatest care. "Choose well
and don't make a mistake," he emphasized, "because in most
cases, the marriage lasts longer than the sentimental connec-
tion. That's why, maybe, if I'd married her, Noelia . . ." And at
the moment he put ellipses on that affirmation, the voice of the
tango singer also fell silent, and as the announcer mentioned
his name and the title of the song, my father, blindly pushing

the faux pearl buttons of the radio, searched until he found the signal that transmitted classical music. In this case, opera. Now it was the grating voice of a tenor that saturated the atmosphere, as I tried to process my father's revelation. If Noelia had been his great past love, one could therefore deduce that my mother had not been, to the same degree. And if this were so, I asked, what had led them to get married, and what united them in the present? "Well," he said, "your mother is a great woman, I don't have any complaints. We've been married for a long time, and when passion ends, love turns into friendship. Your mother is a good companion." Then he got tangled up in a discourse on the subject. Transformations, cycles, advances, setbacks of matrimony . . . all of a sudden, I understood what he was telling me: in his case, the end of love and the passage to conjugal friendship heralded a decision. My father had invited me to accompany him to sound out my reaction to certain decisions, linked to his future. Stated in a clear way: he wanted to let me know through circuitous words that he was thinking of separating from my mother. The words of this indirect communication floated through the heated air of the car, as the vibratos of the tenor, compressed by the poor transmission quality, passed from stridency to interference. Then I could no longer bear the deafening voice in my ears, and said: "Turn this off now or I'll throw myself out of the car." We were moving fast enough that the completion of my promise included a risk of death. My father's astonishment, his laughter at the apparent absurdity of my comment, lasted no more than a second. Then he turned off the radio with a punch of the button, reduced his speed, and using his elbow, lowered the safety latch next to him, which worked for all doors. Looking at me out of the corner of his eye (he wasn't going to stop paying attention to the road either), he asked: "But just what is the matter with you?"

The singer, I now remember, was Mario Lanza. His influence pierced into me like the lance of his surname. If each name hurls a destiny, then I must admit that this singer's, which entered my eardrums like a spear, also penetrated a side of my soul. And it did so at the very moment my father intimated he didn't love my mother and was going to leave us, at the very moment this news so destroyed a part of me that instead of continuing to listen, I'd have preferred to tumble headlong into the road and be flattened by the speeding car behind, at the very moment I also understood he wasn't announcing anything I hadn't already known, but was simply bringing this knowledge into total clarity, high relief: the knowledge that family doesn't exist save for in the illusory effort to construct it and keep it united. And at the same time, only family exists.

The fact is, this paternal sentence about the end of love ruined, in a completely unexpected way and from the very start, the possibility that I would develop full, complex, and mature sentimental relationships. As if my father's decision were a kind of anticipatory sentence, I remained marked by the idea that in the long or short term I would reproduce this model of failure, and so an elemental ethical principle with respect to treatment of the other sex drew me from the beginning away from any serious commitment. Over the years, and perhaps this will last in greater or lesser measure for the rest of my life, I've stuck on my face the frivolous mask of a hyperkinetic Casanova, one who uses and discards woman after woman as if trying to penetrate the bodies of ghosts. And in the end there weren't so very many either, since my fear of hurting the other made me cold in my behavior, and distance isn't the greatest resource if you want to play at amorous conquest, which implies the unfurling of romantic clichés. This distance was thus, at heart, a warning that even I believed it was inconvenient to get involved with me. In my behavior with women, I was a standard bearer of the lesson I'd received: love is what's left out. Now then, to be the best student in an erroneous lesson is no advantage, and my sentimental withdrawal does not eliminate the obvious evidence that my father had been able to explore the territory of possibilities his warning had destroyed in me, since his confession of escape included the story of a past love, failed but existent, as well as the end of another love, which still existed to some degree: the love that united him to my mother, and was being lost in the unbearable duration of the present. And why could he, when I couldn't? Maybe because his own father, my grandfather Ernesto, prudently abstained from initiating him in that sinister knowledge about the fleeting nature of all emotion and the end of all hope. It's clear that when a father is strong, the son must be even more so, and if he cannot be, he has to accept his own weakness, accustom himself to living amidst the ruins until he learns to construct a strength of a different nature and order than that which characterized his predecessor, given that what has been inherited is of no use. Kafka's text can also be read in this sense. He himself writes: "Thus I studied jurisprudence." The *Letter* is a long allegation where the author analyzes his case, places blame, incriminates himself, makes accusations, and adopts the positions of prosecutor, lawyer, executioner, and victim, in accordance with the rhetorical tactic of locating the father in both the chamber of appeal and supreme tribunal. When he is near the end of his discourse, Kafka even pretends to cede his place and take up the possible paternal arguments to wield them against his son, lending his own voice (which could be a shout) to the opponent to arrive at an indubitable truth by means of artifices of the dialectical game. Pure pilpul.

———⭑———

A doctor visits him. She asks his age and date of birth, the day and year in which we are currently living. My father smiles, he doesn't know. The doctor points to me: "And what's his name?" "Him," says my father. I tell the doctor he doesn't know my name anymore, but he recognizes my name when he hears it. Then I say to him: "Dad, what am I called? Roberto?" "No," he says. "Marcos?" "No." "Francisco?" "No." "Mirta?" The doctor jokes: "Maybe by night." My father says: "No." "Daniel?" I ask. "That's the one. That's it." "And who am I? What am I to you?" He looks at me, smiles, opens his hands. "My old man," he says.

———⭑———

"Now, aging father, I treat you better than you treated me when I was a boy." A minor triumph. When it comes down to it, what is there to show here? Satisfaction in pain is loathsome, and my desire to provoke pity combines with my will to appear impartial. But a trap is hidden: a hope that pathos can be a method for the examination of consciousness. Am I writing a literature of denunciation because of the abuse I received in childhood, or a literature of self-denunciation to show how well I accepted the lessons received, to the point that now I can only hold the worst opinions about myself? The world folds like an umbrella, and only the politics of resistance is left to me before the spectacle of his growing incapacity.

I remember the impression reading an episode of the *Aeneid* made on me in adolescence. Virgil tells of how Aeneas, son of Anchises and Aphrodite, flees from a defeated Troy, burning in high Achaean flames. His destiny is not to perish defending his native city, but to lay the foundations of another city, greater and more glorious. During the flight he must carry his father, who is no longer capable of walking on his own. I don't remember the details, except that Aeneas and his men escape in a boat and Anchises never comes to know the Rome his son will found (just as Moses never sets foot in the Promised Land). For me, that scene evokes the image of a vigorous character who bears his father, already ancient or crippled, on his shoulders. Anchises's scrawny legs are wrapped around the chest and neck of his son; the old man's thighs, which in his powerful youth seduced the goddess of love, are now two withered branches. Aeneas moves stealthily in the dark through the lonely night, carrying that weight. As he approaches the water, where the rescue boat is waiting, the ground he treads becomes increasingly muddy, or sandy, making movement difficult. The father's weight deepens their track and slows their advance, and it's not impossible that groups of Achaean victors are moving over the beach in search of Trojan fugitives. Aeneas puts the future of a city and the life of its people at risk to haul the burden of the past. Anchises will die and be buried at Drepana. Now I am a worn out Aeneas carrying an Anchises on his shoulders, and at every moment he weighs more heavily and plunges me deeper into the mud. When my whole body vanishes from the surface (except perhaps my head), he'll leap off and abandon me there.

"Damned is he who feels he cannot speak ill of his parents, for he is not prepared to sacrifice them to make room for his children" (Saint Fermin 11:8).

The truth must be told. He also dreamed of being a writer: he wrote poems, and fragments of a travel diary he once gave me to read and I kept for years without really knowing what to do with it. When he was in a good mood he recited the four best remembered verses from Almafuerte's famous poem:

> *Don't embrace defeat, even when defeated*
> *Don't feel yourself a slave, even when enslaved*
> *Trembling in terror, think yourself fearless*
> *And charge with fury, even when badly wounded*

As long as he could, he asked me to show him the first editions of my books, and gave them back to me with corrections. With a certain fearful respect, he said: "I think here . . . ," and pointed out an involuntary typing error, misplaced comma, or missing period. Attentive to detail, the general sense of the narrative escaped him. But this, which irritated me at the time, did not cease to move me. In his secret dedication, his modest willingness to collaborate, his hidden devotion and concealed pride, he was better and more honest than Don Hermann Kafka, who every time his son handed him a manuscript looking for approval, said: "Leave it for me on the bedside table" and never opened it, or at most answered a few weeks later: "Ah, that . . . No, I still haven't found a moment . . ." Unlike Franz Kafka, and closer to the little Florentine scribe, tonight I do not write so that my father will read me, even if I copy his desire to the letter as an imaginary prolongation of his intention, never made concrete.

Another hospitalization, for bleeding in his urine. If they took away the anticoagulant medicines, maybe the diverticula in his bladder wouldn't open up, but he'd run the risk of his arteries getting plugged, with the prognosticated result of an embolism and an amputated leg or two. He looks at the content of the liquid in his drip bag and wants to control the quantity of the serum, the timing of its fall into the capsule which comes to the tube that brings it to his veins. He also monitors the correct placement of this tube. Observing that the small bit of plastic is slightly bent, he wants to open the channel so that the liquid flows more effectively. A will to survive at all costs. He twists the tube. I tell him: "Don't touch it, you'll pull it out." I say it energetically so he understands, because he's doped. He emerges from the haze, stares at me, and asks: "Are you stupid, or what?!" I don't lower my gaze: "So I'm stupid. You leave that little tube alone because it'll be worse if you pull it out." I leave the room faking anger. I bump into my aunt Alicia, his sister-in-law, who's witnessed the scene. I tell her, laughing: "If he fights, it's because he's not doing so badly." After a while I go back into the room again, in a good mood, ready to make a scene. "So I'm stupid, huh? You ain't gonna talk to me like that! Tell me you're sorry." He looks at me, recognizes the farce: "Enough of this shit!" He laughs, I laugh. I check his tube: the serum is flowing as it should. When he says goodbye, I give him a kiss on each cheek.

The next day, in the afternoon, I go and see him. The señora who takes care of him says: "Tell your son what you told me." My father lifts his hand with the tube and rests it on his chest, or rather the area between his shoulder and clavicle, with the intention of pointing to his heart. Then he points to me: "You. Very loved," he says.

He said the same thing to my sister in the morning. For the first and, I suppose, last time.

The bleeding stops and he goes back to his house. I visit him in the week, under several pretexts: fixing burst PVC pipes, cleaning water tanks. He's sitting down, staring into space. I ask him what's going on. "There's nothing," he says. Then: "I'm old." Then: "When is this going to be sold?" and he points around him. He's never wanted to sell it before. His house, his garden, the place where he's always wanted to be. "If you like, we'll sell it and you can come live closer to me," I tell him. He shrugs. "I'll be able to take you out more often in the chair," I say. He doesn't answer. "Let's play dominoes," I propose. He shrugs, opens the box, spills the pieces onto the table.

A few days later, I pick up the result of the biopsy. Even in the medical jargon, it's clear. When the moment comes, or perhaps before that, now, I'll have to tell him that he was a good father, the best possible father for my sister and for me.

I meet with Silvio Pesarovich, a childhood friend, at a bar. We were both members of I. L. Peretz, a club in Villa Lynch that was part of the Jewish progressive movement, dedicated to forming new generations of countrymen less affiliated with the religion of Yahweh than likely to swell the powerful ranks and control the financial apparatus of the Communist Party. With time, that movement began to disappear. An assimilated Jew— Silvio tells me—doesn't need to belong to a Jewish institution. The Communist Party dissolved within Peronism and what's left to us, smiled my friend, is God (whom he orthodoxically calls HaShem) and the glorious State of Israel.

Silvio wants to talk about literature. I, in contrast, prefer to surrender to the pleasure of pleasures, the complaint. I reel off the time it takes to occupy myself with my father, the economic and moral costs, my battle with the insurance company, the exhaustion of the nurses' constant demands, the intrigues amongst them, their protests and grievances. I predict my own swift ruin, I elaborate on my general feeling of vital extinction. Then I fill him in on the latest medical updates. Silvio interrupts to ask a question I don't quite understand:

"The Maia?" I ask.

"AMIA. Asociación Mutual Israelita Argentina. Have you visited?"

"Me?" I ask. "What for?"

"Because if you pay in advance, when the moment comes to bury your old man in Tablada or Berazategui, they'll give you a 40 percent discount. When my brother died, I didn't know about the markdown and had to shell out 20,000 dollars. If I'd have known, it'd have cost only 12,000."

"I hadn't thought about . . ."

"What hadn't you thought about? You're a Jew, your sister's a Jew, your mother's a Jew, your father's a Jew. Therefore, it's Tablada or Berazategui. Think about it . . ."

A couple weeks later, I'm wandering aimlessly through the Once neighborhood, when all of a sudden I come across the AMIA building. I don't believe in fate, but if chance set me down before its doors, I'd better see what it's all about. The place is a fortress. The security guard asks what I want. "I've come to look into a few services," I say, and clarify: "Burials." He asks to see my document, then lets me pass. I go through a scanner, then a pair of heavy doors. The huge inner patio is dry and dusty, and there's a monument to the victims of the attack, with flags hanging from their countries of origin. The flags are limp, not wrapped around anything. I walk into the central hall. I wonder if everything will explode again right now. I imagine myself alive, hurt, bleeding, trapped, asphyxiated in a tomb of bricks, cement, stone. The dust won't let me breathe and I suffer from claustrophobia . . . I go upstairs in the elevator, which doesn't have mirrors but is lined with a kind of shiny, burnished metal. I put a finger on the metal and press, but it doesn't give way. I get out of the elevator and find a sign for "Community Services." I go to reception. A fat, bearded, middle-aged orthodox Jew typing on his computer attends to me.

"What do you need, love?" he asks, and winks.

I explain, and he asks me to take a seat for a moment. I wait. After a while another orthodox Jew comes out of his office. He wears a kippah, and curly sideburns fall over his temples. He approaches my lover boy. They speak in low voices, but I hear fragments of the conversation. They debate about a chicken or a chicken shop, or a restaurant where chicken is served. The first recommends it, says it's 100 percent kosher, he knows a rabbi who approves it. The second says the chicken may be kosher, but the hands of those who work there are not, and the other foods are far from being kosher . . . To be kosher or not to be kosher, that is, to be a pig. After some time, they say goodbye:

"Chau love."

It seems the sentiment is universal. Love absorbs himself in his computer again, and after a while he raises his head and asks:

"Ashkenazi or Sephardi?"

The start of the romance ends when a bald, skinny guy without a kippah or tefillin approaches. He invites me to come into his office, points toward a chair, asks what I need.

"My father isn't so well," I tell him. "A friend told me there's some paperwork it's advisable to do in advance."

"Your friend is wise," he says, and hands me a printed page. It's a map of the Tablada cemetery, marking out different sectors in yellow, orange, red, purple, green, blue . . .

"Why the division in colors?" I ask.

"By price. Every sector has a different cost."

"And how are they calculated?"

"By proximity to the entrance. The most expensive ones are a block or two away, the least expensive ones are farther out. This one, the violet, has a great price, I recommend you to take a look. It's the affordable section. You have to walk twelve blocks to get there, but it's high demand, not many lots remain . . . It's a steal, 349,000 plus 10 percent in taxes, comes out to 383,900."

"Something like 10,000 dollars at the close of today's stock exchange," I calculate.

"Yes. But if you pay cash there's a 30 percent discount and it comes out to 268,730. I advise you to hurry and leave the advance, because the price of the lots went up last week and I assume they'll go up again next month."

"At the rate of inflation?"

"And what can we do? The advantage is that when the sad moment of the end arrives, the price won't change and the lot will already be reserved. So you don't have to keep thinking about all of this."

"And the cemetery in Berazategui?"

"It comes out to 70,000 pesos."

"Why the difference?"

"Well, Tablada has twenty-five hectares and most families prefer to keep all their dead there so they don't have to move from one cemetery to another on visits. Berazategui has just five hectares, but it's fantastic too. It's a pretty place, very calm, very green."

I go on thinking, remembering the moment we went to bury my paternal grandfather. It was in Tablada. At the entrance they made us go with the coffin into a room that looked like a public restroom, the kind you see in train stations. Tiled walls, wet floor. A big, tall man came to greet us. He was wearing white overalls tucked into rain boots, and a rubber apron that covered his chest and reached to knee level. He held a hose still dripping water. He looked at the coffin, pointed to some metal posts like gymnasts' parallel bars, and told us: "Put it down here and wait outside." Then he turned on the jet of the hose.

We went outside. I asked an employee what that was all about. He explained to me that a Jew, before he is buried, must take a ritual bath. I don't know what kind of ritual could involve hosing down a dead person. I still remember the sound of the water hitting the wood, an almost joyful sound, followed by the deeper and more muffled sound of it pounding against my grandfather's body. And now, as the office worker looks at me, I also remember an article I read a few days ago: at the moment of the preparation of dead Jews' coffins, a hole is made in the lower section and a handful of earth is put inside. Most relatives of the deceased are unaware of this. The detail is symbolic; in this way, supposedly, the body of the dead person can enter into contact more quickly with the earth that will absorb him. The hole is there to ease the labor of the worms. I'm about to tell him: "I can't stand the idea of a body shut away and rotting." But instead I say:

"Are there no other options? Cremation?"

"No! Never!" The guy lifts up his hands. "A Jew is never cremated! Cremation does not exist for a Jew! Except if he has been cremated involuntarily, by some accident."

"Why not?"

"Because the body is the vessel of the soul . . ."

"But when someone dies, doesn't his soul leave his body?"

"Yes, but the body has to be there. If the poor Jew is cremated, where is his soul going to go on the day all bodies rise up, as the Torah predicts? It has to return to the body it left behind."

"And in what state are the bodies going to be that day?"

"The same as they are now," he says. I abstain from asking if by "now" he's referring to our living bodies, or the imprecise "now" of a present of dead bodies in varying states of dissolution, liquefaction, corruption . . . He seems to anticipate my question: "I don't say so, the Torah does."

"I don't believe in God."

"I don't either. But not believing isn't the same as knowing. Believing less still means believing something, in case. That's why a Jew shouldn't be buried in a cemetery of non-Jews. Until he's moved to his cemetery, the dead person will be restless.

So give it a good mulling over. If you bury your father in the Chacarita cemetery, he's going to be restless until you move him to Tablada. If you cremate him, where is his soul going to end up? Floating, nowhere, all over the place, without a destination, without a home where it can return."

I leave the office, I say goodbye to Love who winks at me and waves, I call the elevator, I wait, I think: "If God, YHVH, HaShem, G-d, or whatever the blazes he's called, does truly exist, and his condition to achieving personal immortality is the burial of the Jewish body, then not to do so, to cremate my father, would mean taking a horrible revenge for past wrongs. What would happen to him, adrift, lost forever in the ether? And wouldn't this also condemn my sister and myself to His Fury and Punishment?"

The elevator arrives. What would my father say if he knew that while he's still alive, I'm thinking about the price of his burial? Maybe he'd shrug. "Don't worry about the money," maybe he'd say. I get in and press the button for ground floor. The doors close. There are no mirrors, just those sheets of burnished metal where I rest my forehead and strike it, once, twice, three times before the doors open. My Wailing Wall.

I leave and call Silvio. I tell him:

"I went to the AMIA."

"Did you reserve a lot?"

"No. I asked them. They offered 30 percent."

He laughs.

"You're an idiot. If you'd squeezed a little, you'd have got the forty."

Fire.

———◆———

Earth.

———◆———

Fire
Earth
Fire
Earth
Fire earth fire earth fire earth fire earth
Fire earth fire earth fire earth fire earth
Fire
Earth
Fire
Earth
Fire
Earth
Fire
Earth
Fire
Earth

———◆———

For a while the paracetamol and Buscopan managed to alleviate the pain. Not for long. Tramadol, a low-level opiate, was added. It barely gave him relief for a couple of weeks. In his last blockage, it was impossible to insert a catheter into his arm to drain blood clots, and an opening was cut into his abdomen so the tube would lead directly to the bladder. A few days ago I took him out to his garden, so he could look at the plants. The palliative care doctor forbade me from ever doing so again. He ran the risk of falling, of breaking a bone, of the catheter shifting and giving him a distended bladder. At this point, anyway, he doesn't even get up from bed anymore. He's administered serum through a subcutaneous injection in the shoulder, because his veins are unable to take the pricks. Through the tiny transparent tube, the drops of the last painkiller also slide, the one that will be final. I watch his serenity as he dies. His eyes turn toward me, and I smile with a face that doesn't mean anything. Then his gaze wanders all over the room until his eyelids close. After some time he wakes up. "How are you feeling?" he asks.

I visit him, I say: "You can't go on like this. Get up." "How?" he asks. Despite the opposition of the nurse on duty, I lift him in my arms and sit him in his wheelchair. The body is defenseless, barely clinging to the will to resist. I push the chair, and take along the bar with the bag of hanging serum. We go outside to the garden. He blinks in the afternoon light. "Where are we?" he asks. "Stay here a minute, I'll be back soon," I say. "Okay," he says, and points to something, a rose bush or blackberry tree. Maybe he wants me to cut the grass, trim the hedge, rake the dry leaves. "Wait for me," I say. I go to his room and pick up the syringe. I come back to the garden. It's a golden evening. I don't know what he's looking at anymore. "You'll be okay now," I tell him, dipping the tip of the needle into the serum applicator and pressing down until the plunger can go no further. The morphine begins to circulate. My father seems to nod off, enter a state of calm. All of a sudden he sits upright, pupils shining. It's a shine that competes with the radiance of the world, the same brilliance that animated his eyes when I was a boy and he looked at me with eyes full of scorn. "You're alright now, Dad," I say.

His head falls onto his chest.

It wasn't the first horror film I ever saw, but it's the one that fueled my childhood nightmares. *Mr. Sardonicus* was its name. For years, what I retained of its plot is this summary: an extremely poor peasant who works the land in the middle of nowhere buys a lottery ticket with the hope of changing his luck. A few days later, his father dies and he must give up his best suit, so the dead man can enter the darkness looking sharp. A couple of weeks later, the lottery ticket comes out a winner and the peasant searches for it all over his house, but can't find it. All of a sudden, he remembers he put it in the inner pocket of the jacket the deceased is now wearing. The dilemma: profane the tomb and get rich, or respect the dead man's rest and stay poor.

At night, armed with a shovel and lantern, he goes to the town cemetery, digs up the coffin and opens it. What he didn't foresee is that the corruption of the corpse would already have begun its work, so the face of his father is deformed into a horrifying rictus, the muscles of the cheeks pulling the lips upward to expose the teeth in a kind of sardonic grimace. The peasant gives a cry of horror, an extreme spine-tingling cry that stretches and deforms his muscles. Now he is a millionaire, but his face stays fixed as a reflection of the paternal sneer.

———

Kafka never understood the nature of paternal affection, of shame as a mask. Who told him his father never read his writing? Where did he get the idea that the best way to read a son is to read the books the son writes? Every few years, the publisher who edits most of my books sends a note saying I can now withdraw "excess copies," that is, the copies of my books that haven't sold, and that otherwise will be sent off to be pulped. Once, since I didn't have any place to store them, I sent a few boxes to my father's house. In those days he could still walk, at least to take a turn around the block.

A few days later, Elvira, the weekend nurse, told me my father had asked her to bring along some copies, and they'd gone from house to house leaving them in front of doors and garages, and inside neighbors' postboxes. My father had no reason to read me, but giving away his son's books was a way of showing his love.

———

Five days before dying, he soliloquized his end, lulled into a morphine dream. I don't know what he was talking about, but at some point he named my mother. "Malvina," he said. It was strange, because over the last few years he'd forgotten her name.

He referred to her as "wife," "the wife." But this time he said: "Malvina." I asked if he wanted to see her. "Yes," he said. "Who?" I asked. "Malvina." "You want her to come?" "Yes," he said.

I didn't call my mother.

Two days before he died, Elvira took my father's hand, brought it to her lips, and kissed it. He was unconscious, but he grabbed Elvira's hand, pressed it against his own lips and kissed it. "Don Luis," she said. "Don Luis."

I looked away.

Later Elvira told me: "Your father was a grouch, but I won't forget that gesture of his until the day I die."

There he is, stretched out, in death rattles. His eyes are closed, his chest rises up with the struggle of each breath. The hoarse wheezing of the end. I call for the doctor to come and inject him, to end the agony, but no one answers. I'll do it, I thought, I'll be the one who ends it. But there isn't enough time. I clutch his hand and talk to him: "Dad," I say, "we're all here, your children, your grandchildren, we all love you." Then he gives a final heave and is still. The eyes close, the expression twists. The face. The gob, the mug. The teeth, protruding. The weekday nurse comes in and asks: "Is he . . ." "Yes." "And now . . . ?"

Now, nothing. Now there is nothing left to do.

The end of a life well lived shouldn't be solely a cause for lament. Within a closed room, in the area where the wakes take place, the rabbi explains the mourning rituals. He talks for long enough to ensure that the children won't be there the moment the employees take away the coffin with their father's body, to hoist it, squeaking, onto the funeral cart.

Exit. Some people walking by the procession make a distracted sign of the cross. The avenue is wide. After the countryside of Vélez Sarsfield we reach the area controlled by Nueva Chicago football club. Side streets, modest houses. The city of the dead is a city of low tombstones, mostly black marble, with the names of the deceased and their dates of birth and death, just barely visible. The cart with the coffin has to be pushed by male relatives, but it's unusual for a son to take one of the handles. The heat is devastating and forces a slow pace. At last we reach the shaft at the end, in a lost corner of this metropolis of the afterlife. The son's girlfriend wants to know if the ceremony will be short or long. A nephew points to the coffin: "For my uncle it will be eternal," he says. The rabbi asks if someone will take part in the ritual rending of a garment. The daughter accepts a snip, the son the tearing of his shirt. Then he says to the rabbi: "You owe me 450 pesos." The rabbi doesn't seem to enjoy this display of humor. The daughter sings a Yiddish song in a low voice, resting her hand on the dark mantle with the six-pointed star. They lay the coffin at the bottom, and the beautiful granddaughter tosses in some flowers plucked from her grandfather's garden. Pain has no end, but it's time to go. We walk in the sun, without the comfort of Jehovah's hand, because as it has been known since the time of the Holocaust, the Lord of the Jews is absence. Goodbye, Dad.

As I began to say before, when my father was a boy, he accompanied his own father, my grandfather Ernesto, to his job. Ernesto was a porter at the Israelite Hospital and was also in charge of eliminating the remains from surgeries. Organs, amputations, limbs, tumors. He had to carry them in a bucket and take them to the crematorium, and sometimes he'd make the trip crying. Maybe my own father told me this. And maybe it was to avoid seeing his dad cry, a way of crying that was identical to his own, that he moved away from that career path as a young boy and instead played at being an elevator operator. "What floor?" Dad would ask those going up, and press the button. When they arrived at the floor indicated, he'd stretch out a hand waiting for money, as payment for service. When he received the centavos he'd flick them into the air, to make them shine and spin, and then catch them and tuck them into the pockets of his short pants.

Years later, while carrying a red flag in an act of opposition to the Peronist government, some mounted police entered at a gallop; a policeman lifted his club and gave him a blow to the head that knocked him out. The blow left an internal wound, a callus that put pressure on an area of his brain that generated electrical shocks. If he didn't take medication, his mind could go blank for seconds at a time, a disconnect on the verge of fainting and epilepsy. "Everything is Perón's fault," he'd sometimes say with a laugh.

Everything has its consequences in this world. In his last days, even when his difficulty speaking increased, he somehow made himself understood. After he died, Elvira told me that with half words he always insisted he'd buried a few gold coins somewhere. I think it was his way of invoking the moments when he'd press the elevator button, then reach out his hand to receive those precious centavos, with their gleam of life.

—◆—

Father. I wrote these pages, an unveiling and shroud, so that you survive in some way.

Mother. I wrote these pages, an unveiling and shroud, so that you understand my anger and desire for reconciliation.

—◆—

Throughout all of our first years of life, Chuchi—my sister Claudia—and I slept in the same room. After my mother or father turned out the light, I wished her good night by saying, for example: "Sweet dreams," before she answered: "Sweet dreams." For some reason, maybe just because I was the older brother, I thought I had to have the last word, so I completed her answer by saying: "Sleep well." To that, she added: "You too." From that moment, a battle began for the right to close the dialogue. It was a dispute in which Claudia showed an iron will. The tone elevated: "You be quiet." "No, you be quiet." "You first." "No, you first." "No, you first." "I talked first." "You talked first but I talked last." "Okay, but I'm talking now." "Shhh, enough." "You, shhh." "Stop talking." "I'll be quiet when you do." "I was the one who said to be quiet first . . ." And so on, in a progression that made the hairs on my neck bristle. I don't think anyone has ever irritated me as much as my sister has, for which I'm very grateful. The fact is that over the course of those nights, when I was always the one who first surrendered to silence, I discovered a way to compensate for my loss, by projecting myself into the adventures of the great life I dreamed I was destined for, imitating the adventures of the heroes of the books I read. But after a while I wore out this technique, and since sleep still didn't come, instead of those consolations of the imagination I found myself prisoner to the threats of insomnia. Ghosts waited in the darkness, rising up in the shadows with every creak of the wooden furniture, and there was no way to flee because the bed itself was protection: By faking death, the dragons and reptiles would mistake the lump of my body for the folds of sheets and blankets. By contrast, if I moved a foot out from under the blankets and rested it on the ground, I'd become visible and vulnerable, defenseless. So I curled up, tucked my head under the covers and tried to go unnoticed, covering my eyelids with my fingers to stop their inner light from guiding any monsters my way that would like to gobble me up. The best way to hide that light was to press my eyeballs little by little, with increasing force: the tips of the fingers applied their pressure, easing or condensing it into the depths of the pupils. In a few seconds, the irritated optic nerve began to flare with magenta rays, tiny formations, electric explosions, yellows that turned green, circles that absorbed other circles, evanescent, complex designs and shimmerings. The thumb on the left eye, the tips of the index and middle fingers on the right, pressed down. And thus they arrived in masses, a dazzling blindness: the stars. They dissolved and combined, turning upon themselves, as I, though dominated by terror, swelled with happiness witnessing the forms of the Universe.

BEYOND THE LAW

Translator's Note

Daniel Guebel begins The Jewish Son *by writing: "An anecdote can explain everything, if you don't forget what escapes it." Further on, he says: "An anecdote can explain everything, if you add back what escapes it." The transition from "don't forget" to "add back," from the passive to the active voice, suggests (even if it does not encapsulate) the journey to becoming a writer.*

FIRST PETITIONER

You, who come from honey and sand, from patios and carob trees, from fields and open skies, still believe in the Law. You ask to pass through the door. The guardian says: "Later." If you were to come in, says the guardian, you would find only another guardian, then another, more powerful. And thus to infinity. So you do not enter. You stay at the door, patient, without crossing the threshold. Time passes. You look at the guardian with his fur coat, big nose, and black beard, and wait for permission. You stay seated for many years, and answer his questions, despite the obvious indifference. Not yet, not yet, not yet. You pass him some bills he accepts only to please you, also evident. You become obsessed with this guardian, start to think he is all that matters. Your vision blurs and narrows to a tunnel. You find yourself speaking to the flea on his coat. Is the darkness outside or in your mind? Yet there is a glow behind the door, a promise. An initial radiance. Your experiences condense into a hard kernel; everything becomes the guardian standing before this radiance. He is your father, your son, your daughter, your mother. You curl into a ball, smaller each day, and the guard shouts, and you do not understand, and he shouts louder. No one else had permission, only you could have entered. But you did not go at the right time. And now the door is closed forever.

(In this philosophical tradition, if you come to a definite conclusion, you have made a mistake. Another reading is always possible. Don't forget you are present for somebody else, the one behind the threshold, who does not enter. And the radiance of your shining body seeps under the door, and the other, curled into a ball, falls in love with your dying light.)

SECOND PETITIONER

You see light on the other side of the door, and want to reach it, become that freedom. Maybe there was a time when you yourself were light, but now you are a longing shard. Waiting for light, filling out paperwork to reach it or become it, in rejection of absence. Transparent, ethereal, a passage between worlds. Music, or clear rules. You seek to become the Law, even